Poul Anderson (1926-2001) was born in Pennsylvania of Scandinavian parents and lived for a short time in Denmark before the outbreak of World War II. He attended the University of Minnesota and gained a degree in physics in 1948. He joined the Minneapolis Fantasy Society and associated with such writers as Gordon R. Dickson and Clifford D. Simak, and published his first science fiction story, 'Tomorrow's Children', which he wrote with F. N. Waldrop, in 1947. Among his many fine novels are *Brain Wave*, *Three Hearts and Three Lions*, *War of the Wing-Men*, *Mirkheim*, *People of the Wind* and *The Avatar*. He was President of the Science Fiction Writers of America 1972–3, won the Gandalf (Grand Master) Award for 1977, and received seven Hugos and three Nebulas for his shorter fiction.

'Fascinating ... strikingly well conceived ... convincingly sustained'
The Encyclopedia of Science Fiction

'An enjoyable novel about the relativistic effects on the space-ship Leonora Christine and its crew as it approaches the speed of light and becomes as big as the universe ... The voyage through space-time takes the ship beyond the dissolution of our universe'
Brian W. Aldiss

Vault of the Ages (1952)
Brain Wave (1954)
No World of their Own (1955)
Planet of No Return (1956)
Star Ways (1956)
The Snows of Ganymede (1958)
War of the Wing-Men (1958)
The Enemy Stars (1959)
Perish by the Sword (1959)
Virgin Planet (1959)
Earthman, Go Home (1960)
The Golden Slave (1960)
The High Crusade (1960)
Murder in Black Letter (1960)
Rogue Sword (1960)
Three Hearts and Three Lions (1961)
Mayday Orbit (1961)
Orbit Unlimited (1961)
Twilight World (1961)
After Doomsday (1962)
The Makeshift Rocket (1962)
Murder Bound (1962)
Let the Spaceman Beware (1963)
Shield (1963)
Guardians of Time (1965)
The Star Fox (1965)
Time and Stars (1965)
The Fox, the Dog, and the Griffin (1966)
Ensign Flandry (1966)
The Rebel Worlds (1966)
World Without Stars (1966)
The Horn of Time (1968)
Beyond the Beyond (1969)
Satan's World (1969)
A Circus of Hells (1970)
Tales of the Flying Mountains (1970)
The Byworlder (1971)
The Dancer from Atlantis (1971)

Operation Chaos (1971)
There Will Be Time (1972)
Hrolf Kraki's Saga (1973)
The People of the Wind (1973)
The Queen of Air and Darkness (1973)
The Day of Their Return (1974)
A Knight of Ghosts and Shadows (1974)
Fire Time (1974)
A Midsummer Tempest (1974)
Inheritors of the Earth with Gordon Eklund (1974)
Star Prince Charlie with Gordon R. Dickson (1975)
Homeward and Beyond (1976)
Inheritors of Earth (1976)
The Winter of the World (1976)
Agent of the Terran Empire (1977)
Mirkheim (1977)
A World Named Cleopatra (1977)
The Avatar (1978)
The Peregrine (1978)
The Demon of Scattery (1979)
Earthman's Burden (1979)
Flandry of Terra (1979)
The Merman's Children (1979)
A Stone in Heaven (1979)
The Devil's Game (1980)
The Golden Horn (1980)
The Road of the Sea Horse (1980)
The Sign of the Raven (1980)
Explorations (1981)
Fantasy (1981)
Winners (1981)
Cold Victory (1982)
The Gods Laughed (1982)
Maurai and Kith (1982)
New America (1982)
The Long Night (1983)
Orion Shall Rise (1983)

Time Patrolman (1983)
Seven Conquests (1984)
The Games of Empire (1985)
Roma Mater with Karen Anderson (1986)
Dahut with Karen Anderson (1988)
The Dog and the Wolf with Karen Anderson (1988)
The Year of the Ransom (1988)
The Boat of a Million Years (1989)
No Truce with Kings (1989)
Alight in the Void (1991)
How to Build a Planet with Stephen W. Gillett (1991)
Inconstant Star (1991)
Kinship with the Stars (1991)
The Longest Voyage (1991)
The Time Patrol (1991)
Flandry (1993)
Harvest of Stars (1993)
The Stars Are Also Fire (1994)
Game of Empire (1994)
All One Universe (1996)
The Fleet of Stars (1997)
Harvest the Fire (1997)
The Saturn Game (1997)
War of the Gods (1997)

Starfarers (1998)
Operation Luna (1999)
Genesis (2000)
Hokas Pokas with Gordon R. Dickson (2000)
Mother of Kings (2001)

SHORT STORY COLLECTIONS
Stranger from Earth (1961)
Trader to the Stars (1966)
The Trouble Twister (1966)
The Book of Poul Anderson (1975)
The Best of Poul Anderson (1976)
The Earth Book of Stormgate (1978)
Operations Otherworld (1983)
Past Times (1984)
The Unicorn Trade with Karen Anderson (1984)
Dialogue with Darkness (1985)
The King of YS with Karen Anderson (1987)
Space Folk (1989)
The Shield of Time (1990)
The Armies of Elfland (1992)
The Imperial Stars (2000)

SF MASTERWORKS

TAU ZERO

Poul Anderson

Copyright © Poul Anderson 1970
All rights reserved

The right of Poul Anderson to be identified as the author
of this work has been asserted by him in accordance with
the Copyright, Designs and Patents Act 1988.

A short version of this novel appeared in Galaxy Science Fiction
for June and August 1967 under the title 'To Outlive Eternity',
Copyright © 1967 by Galaxy Publishing Corporation

This edition published in Great Britain in 2006 by
Gollancz
An imprint of the Orion Publishing Group
Orion House, 5 Upper St Martin's Lane.
London WC2H 9EA

An Hachette Livre UK company

1 1

A CIP catalogue record for this book
is available from the British Library

ISBN 978 0 57507 732 4

Printed and bound by Clays Ltd, Elcograf S.p.A.

The Orion Publishing Group's policy is to use papers that
are natural, renewable and recyclable products and made
from wood grown in sustainable forests. The logging and
manufacturing processes are expected to conform to the
environment regulations of the country of origin.

www.orionbooks.co.uk

CHAPTER 1

'Look – there – rising over the Hand of God. Is it?'

'Yes, I think so. Our ship.'

They were the last to go as Millesgården was closed. Most of that afternoon they had wandered among the sculptures, he awed and delighted by his first experience of them, she bidding an unspoken farewell to what had been more a part of her life than she had understood until now. They were lucky in the weather, when summer was waning. This day on Earth had been sunlight, breezes that made leaf shadows dance on the villa walls, a clear sound of fountains.

But when the sun went down, the garden seemed abruptly to come still more alive. It was as if the dolphins were tumbling through their waters, Pegasus storming skyward, Folke Filbyter peering after his lost grandson while his horse stumbled in the ford, Orpheus listening, the young sisters embracing in their resurrection – all unheard, because this was a single instant perceived, but the time in which these figures actually moved was no less real than the time which carried men.

'As if they were alive, bound for the stars, and we must stay behind and grow old,' Ingrid Lindgren murmured.

Charles Reymont didn't hear her. He stood on the flagstones under a birch tree, whose leaves rustled and had begun very faintly to turn color, and looked toward *Leonora Christine*. Atop its pillar, the Hand of God upbearing the Genius of Man lifted in silhouette against a greenish-blue dusk. Behind it, the tiny rapid star crossed and sank again.

'Are you sure that wasn't an ordinary satellite?' Lindgren asked through quietness. 'I never expected we'd see – '

Reymont cocked a brow at her. 'You're the first officer, and you don't know where your own vessel is or what she's

7

doing?' His Swedish had a choppy accent, like most of the languages he spoke, that underlined the sardonicism.

'I'm not the navigation officer,' she said, defensive. 'Also, I put the whole matter out of my mind as much as I can. You should do the same. We'll spend plenty of years with it.' She half reached toward him. Her tone gentled. 'Please. Don't spoil this evening.'

Reymont shrugged. 'Pardon me. I didn't mean to.'

An attendant neared, stopped, and said deferentially: 'I am sorry, we must shut the gates now.'

'Oh!' Lindgren started, glanced at her watch, looked over the terraces. They were empty of everything except the life that Carl Milles had shaped into stone and metal, three centuries ago. 'Why, why, it's far past closing time. I hadn't realized.'

The attendant bowed. 'Since my lady and gentleman obviously wished it, I let them alone after the other visitors left.'

'You know us, then,' Lindgren said.

'Who does not?' The attendant's gaze admired her. She was tall and well formed, regular of features, blue eyes set wide, blond hair bobbed just under the ears. Her civilian garments were more stylish than was common on a space-woman; the rich soft colors and flowing draperies of neomedieval suited her.

Reymont contrasted. He was a stocky, dark, hard-countenanced man who had never bothered to have removed the scar that seamed his brow. His plain tunic and trews might as well have been a uniform.

'Thank you for not pestering us,' he said, more curt than cordial.

'I took for granted you wished freedom from being a celebrity,' the attendant replied. 'No doubt many others recognized you too but felt likewise.'

'You'll find we Swedes are a courteous people.' Lindgren smiled at Reymont.

'I won't argue that,' her companion said. 'Nobody can help running into it, when you're everywhere in the Solar System.' He paused. 'But then, whoever steers the world

8

had better be polite. The Romans were in their day. Pilate, for instance.'

The attendant was taken aback at the implied rebuff. Lindgren declared a little sharply, 'I said *älskvärdig*, not *artig*.' ('Courteous,' not 'polite'.) She offered her hand. 'Thank you, sir.'

'My pleasure, Miss First Officer Lindgren,' the attendant answered. 'May you have a fortunate voyage and come home safe.'

'If the voyage is really fortunate,' she reminded him, 'we will never come home. If we do – ' She broke off. He would be in his grave. 'Again I thank you,' she said to the little middle-aged man. 'Good-by,' she said to the gardens.

Reymont exchanged a clasp too and mumbled something. He and Lindgren went out.

High walls darkened the nearly deserted pavement beyond. Footfalls sounded hollow. After a minute the woman remarked, 'I do wonder if that was our ship we saw. We're in a high latitude. And not even a Bussard vessel is big and bright enough to shine through sunset glow.'

'She is when the scoopfield webs are extended,' Reymont told her. 'And she was moved into a skewed orbit yesterday, as part of her final tests. They'll take her back to the ecliptic plane before we depart.'

'Yes, of course, I've seen the program. But I've no reason to remember exactly who is doing what with her at which time. Especially when we aren't leaving for another two months. Why should you keep track?'

'When I'm simply the constable.' Reymont's mouth bent into a grin. 'Let's say that I'm practicing to be a worrywart.'

She glanced sideways at him. The look became a scrutiny. They had emerged on an esplanade by the water. Across it, Stockholm's lights were kindling, one by one, as night grew upward among houses and trees. But the channel remained almost mirrorlike, and as yet there were few sparks in heaven save Jupiter. You could still see without help.

Reymont hunkered down and drew their hired boat in. Bond anchors secured the lines to the concrete. He had obtained a special license to park practically anywhere. An interstellar expedition was that big an event. Lindgren and he had spent the morning in a cruise around the Archipelago – a few hours amidst greenness, homes like parts of the islands whereon they grew, sails and gulls and sunglitter across waves. Little of that would exist at Beta Virginis, and none of it in the distances between.

'I am beginning to feel what a stranger you are to me, Carl,' she said slowly. 'To everyone?'

'Eh? My biography's on record.' The boat bumped against the esplanade. Reymont sprang down into its cockpit. Holding the line taut with one hand, he offered her the other. She had no need to lean heavily on him as she descended, but did. His arm scarcely stirred beneath her weight.

She sat down on a bench next the wheel. He twisted the screw top of the anchor he grasped. Intermolecular binding forces let go with a faint smacking noise that answered the slap-slap of water on hull. His movements could not be called graceful, as hers were, but they were quick and economical.

'Yes, I suppose we've all memorized each other's official accounts.' She nodded. 'For you, the absolute minimum you could get by with telling."

(Charles Jan Reymont. Citizenship status, Interplanetarian. Thirty-four years old. Born in the Antarctic, but not one of its better colonies; the sublevels of Polyugorsk offered only poverty and turbulence to a boy whose father had died early. The youth he became got to Mars by some unspecified means and held a variety of jobs till the troubles broke out. Then he fought with the Zebras, with such distinction that afterward the Lunar Rescue Corps offered him a berth. There he completed his academic education and rose fast in rank, until as colonel he had much to do with improving the police branch. When he applied for this expedition, the Control Authority was glad to accept him.)

'Nothing whatsoever of yourself,' Lindgren observed. 'Did you even give that away in the psychological testing?'

Reymont had gone forward and cast off the bow line. He

stowed both anchors neatly, took the wheel, and started the motor. The magnetic drive was soundless and the propeller made scant noise, but the boat slipped rapidly outward. He kept his eyes straight ahead. 'Why do you care?' he asked.

'We'll be together for a number of years. Quite possibly for the rest of our lives.'

'It makes me wonder why you spent today with me, then.'

'You invited me.'

'After you gave me a call at my hotel. You must have checked with the crew registry to find where I was.'

Millesgården vanished in swift-deepening darkness aft. Lights along the channel, and from the inner city beyond, did not show whether she flushed. Her face turned from him, though. 'I did,' she admitted. 'I . . . thought you might be lonely. You have no one, have you?'

'No relatives left. I'm only touring the fleshpots of Earth. Won't be any where we are bound.'

Her sight lifted again, toward Jupiter this time, a steady tawny-white lamp. More stars were treading forth. She shivered and drew her cloak tight around her, against the autumnal air. 'No,' she said mutedly. 'Everything alien. And when we've hardly begun to map, to understand, that world yonder – our neighbor, our sister – to cross thirty-two light-years – '

'People are like that.'

'Why are you going, Carl?'

His shoulders lifted and dropped. 'Restless, I suppose. And frankly, I made enemies in the Corps. Rubbed them the wrong way, or outdistanced them for promotion. I was at the point where I couldn't advance further without playing office politics. Which I despise.' His glance met hers. Both lingered a moment. 'You?'

She sighed. 'Probably sheer romanticism. Ever since I was a child, I thought I must go to the stars, the way a prince in a fairy tale must go to Elf Land. At last, by insisting to my parents, I got them to let me enroll in the Academy.'

His smile held more warmth than usual. 'And you made

an outstanding record in the interplanetary service. They didn't hesitate to make you first officer of your first extrasolar ship.'

Her hands fluttered in her lap. 'No. Please. I'm not bad at my work. But it's easy for a woman to rise fast in space. She's in demand. And my job on *Leonora Christine* will be essentially executive. I'll have more to do with . . . well, human relations . . . than astronautics.'

He returned his vision forward. The boat was rounding the land, headed into Saltsjön. Water traffic thickened. Hydrofoils whirred past. A cargo submarine made her stately way toward the Baltic. Overhead, air taxis flitted like fireflies. Central Stockholm was a many-colored unrestful fire and a thousand noises blent into one somehow harmonious growl.

'That brings me back to my question.' Reymont chuckled. 'My counter-question, rather, since you were pressing in on me. Don't think I haven't enjoyed your company. I did, much, and if you'll have dinner with me I'll consider this day among the better ones of my life. But most of our gang scattered like drops of mercury the minute our training period ended. They're deliberately avoiding their shipmates. Better spend the time with those they'll never see again. You, now – you have roots. An old, distinguished, well-to-do family; an affectionate one, I gather; father and mother alive, brothers, sisters, cousins, surely anxious to do everything they can for you in the few weeks that remain. Why did you leave them today?'

She sat unspeaking.

'Your Swedish reserve,' he said after a while. 'Appropriate to the rulers of mankind. I ought not to have intruded. Just give me the same right of privacy, will you?'

And presently: 'Would you like to join me at dinner? I've found quite a decent little live-service restaurant.'

'Yes,' she answered. 'Thank you. I would.'

She rose to stand beside him, laying one hand on his arm. The thick muscles stirred beneath her fingers. 'Don't call us rulers,' she begged. 'We aren't. That's what the whole idea was behind the Covenant. After the nuclear war . . . that close a brush with world death . . . something had to be done.'

'Uh-huh,' he grunted. 'I've read an occasional history book myself. General disarmament; a world police force to maintain it; *sed quis custodiet ipsos Custodes?* Who can we trust with a monopoly of the planet killer weapons and unlimited powers of inspection and arrest? Why, a country big and modern enough to make peace keeping a major industry; but not big enough to conquer anyone else or force its will on anyone without the support of a majority of nations; and reasonably well thought of by everyone. In short, Sweden.'

'You do understand, then,' she said happily.

'I do. Including the consequences. Power feeds on itself, not by conspiracy, but by logical necessity. The money the world pays, to underwrite the cost of the Control Authority, passes through here; therefore you become the richest country on Earth, with all that that implies. And the diplomatic center, goes without saying. And when every reactor, spaceship, laboratory is potentially dangerous and must be under the Authority, that means some Swede has a voice in everything that matters. And this leads to your being imitated, even by those who no longer like you. Ingrid, my friend, your people can't help turning into new Romans.'

Her gladness drooped. 'Don't *you* like us, Carl?'

'As well as anybody, considering. You've been humane masters to date. Too humane, I'd say. In my own case, I ought to be grateful, since you allow me to be essentially a stateless person, which I think I prefer. No, you've not done badly.' He gestured toward the towers down which radiance cataracted, to right and left. 'It won't last, anyhow.'

'What do you mean?'

'I don't know. I'm only certain that nothing is forever. No matter how carefully you design a system, it will go bad and die.'

Reymont stopped to choose words. 'In your case,' he said, 'I believe the end may come from this very stability you take pride in. Has anything important changed, on

Earth at least, since the late twentieth century? Is that a desirable state of affairs?

'I suppose,' he added, 'that's one reason for planting colonies in the galaxy, if we can. Against Ragnarok.'

Her fists clenched. Her face turned upward again. The night was now entire, but few stars could be seen through the veil of light over the city. Elsewhere – in Lapland, for instance, where her parents had a summer cottage – they would shine unmercifully sharp and many.

'I'm being a poor escort,' Reymont apologized. 'Let's get off these schoolboy profundities and discuss more interesting subjects. Like an aperitif.'

Her laugh was uncertain.

He managed to keep the talk inconsequential while he nosed into Strömmen, docked the boat, and led her on foot across the bridge to Old Town. Beyond the royal palace they found themselves under softer illumination, walking down narrow streets between high golden-hued buildings that had stood much as they were for several hundred years. Tourist season was past; of the uncounted foreigners in the city, few had reason to visit this enclave; except for an occasional pedestrian or electrocyclist, Reymont and Lindgren were nearly alone.

'I shall miss this,' she said.

'It's picturesque,' he conceded.

'More than that, Carl. It's not just an outdoor museum. Real human beings live here. And the ones who were before them, they stay real too. In, oh, Birger Jarl's Tower, the Riddarholm Church, the shields in the House of Nobles, the Golden Peace where Bellman drank and sang – It's going to be lonely in space, Carl, so far from our dead.'

'Nevertheless you're leaving.'

'Yes. Not easily. My mother who bore me, my father who took me by the hand and led me out to teach me constellations. Did he know what he was doing to me that night?' She drew a breath. 'That's partly why I got in touch with you. I had to escape from what I'm doing to them. If only for a single day.'

'You need a drink,' he said, 'and here we are.'

14

The restaurant fronted on the Great Marketplace. Between the surrounding steep façades you could imagine how knights had clattered merrily across the paving stones. You did not remember how the gutters ran with blood and heads were stacked high during a certain winter week, for that was long past and men seldom dwell on the hurts that befell other men. Reymont conducted Lindgren to a table in a candlelit room which they had to themselves, and ordered akvavit with beer chasers.

She matched him drink for drink, though she had less mass and less practice. The meal that followed was lengthy even by Scandinavian standards, with considerable wine during it and considerable cognac afterward. He let her do most of the talking.

– of a house near Drottningholm, whose park and gardens were almost her own; sunlight through windows, gleaming over burnished wood floors and on silver that had been passed down for ten generations; a sloop on the lake, heeled to the wind, her father at the tiller with a pipe in his teeth, her hair blowing loose; monstrous nights at wintertime, and in their middle that warm cave named Christmas; the short light nights of summer, the balefires kindled on St. John's Eve that had once been lit to welcome Baldr home from the underworld; a walk in the rain with a first sweetheart, the air cool, drenched with water and odor of lilacs; travels around Earth, the Pyramids, the Parthenon, Paris at sunset from the top of Montparnasse, the Taj Mahal, Angkor Wat, the Kremlin, the Golden Gate Bridge, yes, and Fujiyama, the Grand Canyon, Victoria Falls, the Great Barrier Reef –

– of love and merriment at home but discipline too, order, gravity in the presence of strangers; music around, Mozart the dearest; a fine school, where teachers and classmates brought a complete new universe exploding into her awareness; the Academy, harder work than she had known she could do, and how pleased she was to discover she was able; cruises through space, to the planets, oh, she had stood on the snows of Titan with Saturn overhead, stunned by beauty; always, always her kindred to return to –

– in a good world, its people, their doings, their pleasures all good; yes, there remained problems, outright cruelties, but those could be solved in time through reason and good will; it would be a joy to believe in some kind of religion, since that would perfect the world by giving it ultimate purpose, but in the absence of convincing proof she could still do her best to help supply that meaning, help mankind move toward something loftier –

– but no, she wasn't a prig, he mustn't believe that; in fact, she often wondered if she wasn't too hedonistic, a bit more liberated than was best; however, she did get fun out of life without hurting anyone else, as far as she could tell; she lived with high hopes.

Reymont poured the last coffee for her. The waiter had finally brought the bill, though he seemed in no more hurry to collect than most of his kind in Stockholm. 'I expect that in spite of the drawbacks,' Reymont said, 'you'll manage to enjoy our voyage.'

Her voice had gotten a bit slurred. Her eyes, regarding him, stayed bright and level. 'I plan to,' she declared. 'That's the main reason I called you. Remember, during training I urged you to come here for part of your furlough.' By now they were using the intimate pronoun.

Reymont drew on his cigar. Smoking would be prohibited in space, to avoid overloading the life support systems, but tonight he could still put a blue cloud in front of him.

She leaned forward, laying a hand over his free one on the table. 'I was thinking ahead,' she told him. 'Twenty-five men and twenty-five women. Five years in a metal shell. Another five years if we turn back immediately. Even with antisenescence treatments, a decade is a big piece out of a life.'

He nodded.

'And of course we'll stay to explore,' she went on. 'If that third planet is habitable, we'll stay to colonize – forever – and we'll start having children. Whatever we do, there are going to be liaisons. We'll pair off.'

He said, low lest it seem too blunt: 'You think you and I might make a couple?'

16

'Yes.' Her tone strengthened. 'It may seem immodest of me, whether or not I am a spacewoman. But I'll be busier than most, the first several weeks of travel especially. I won't have time for nuances and rituals. It could end with me in a situation I don't want. Unless I think ahead and make preparations. As I'm doing.'

He lifted her hand to his lips. 'I am deeply honored, Ingrid. Though we may be too unlike.'

'No, I suspect that's what draws me.' Her palm curved around his mouth and slid down his cheek. 'I want to know you. You are more a man than any I've met before.'

He counted money onto the bill. It was the first time that she had seen him move not entirely steadily. He ground out his cigar, watching it as he did. 'I'm staying at a hotel over on Tyska Brinken,' he said. 'Rather shabby.'

'I don't mind,' she answered. 'I doubt if I'll notice.'

CHAPTER 2

Seen from one of the shuttles that brought her crew to her, *Leonora Christine* resembled a dagger pointed at the stars.

Her hull was a conoid, tapering toward the bow. Its burnished smoothness seemed ornamented rather than broken by the exterior fittings. These were locks and hatches; sensors for instruments; housings for the two boats that would make the planet-falls for which she herself was not designed; and the web of the Bussard drive, now folded flat. The base of the conoid was quite broad, since it contained the reaction mass among other things; but the length was too great for this to be particularly noticeable.

At the top of the dagger blade, a structure fanned out which you might have imagined to be the guard of a basket hilt. Its rim supported eight skeletal cylinders pointing aft. These were the thrust tubes, that acclerated the reaction mass backward when the ship moved at merely inter-planetary speeds. The 'basket' enclosed their controls and power plant.

Beyond this, darker in hue, extended the haft of the dagger, ending finally in an intricate pommel. The latter was the Bussard engine; the rest was shielding against its radiation when it should be activated.

Thus *Leonora Christine*, seventh and youngest of her class. Her outward simplicity was required by the nature of her mission and was as deceptive as a human skin; inside, she was very nearly as complex and subtle. The time since the basic idea of her was first conceived, in the middle twentieth century, had included perhaps a million man-years of thought and work directed toward achieving the reality; and some of those men had possessed intellects equal to any that had ever existed. Though practical experience and essential tools had already been gotten when construction was begun upon her, and though technological civilization had reached its fantastic flowering (and finally, for a while, was not burdened by war or the threat of war) – neverthe-less, her cost was by no means negligible, had indeed provoked widespread complaint. All this, to send fifty people to one practically next-door star?

Right. That's the size of the universe.

It loomed behind her, around her, where she circled Earth. Staring away from sun and planet, you saw a crystal darkness huger than you dared comprehend. It did not appear totally black; there light reflections within your eyeballs, if nowhere else; but it was the final night, that our kindly sky holds from us. The stars thronged it, unwinking, their brilliance winter-cold. Those sufficiently luminous to be seen from the ground showed their colors clear in space: steel-blue Vega, golden Capella, ember of Betelgeuse. And if you were not trained, the lesser members of the galaxy that had become visible were so many as to drown the familiar constellations. The night was wild with suns.

And the Milky Way belted heaven with ice and silver; and the Magellanic Clouds were not vague shimmers but roiling and glowing; and the Andromeda galaxy gleamed sharp across more than a million light-years; and you felt your soul drowning in those depths and hastily pulled your vision back to the snug cabin that held you.

Ingrid Lindgren entered the bridge, caught a handhold, and poised in mid-air. 'Reporting for duty, Mr Captain,' she announced formally.

Lars Telander turned about to greet her. In free fall, his gaunt and gawky figure became lovely to watch, like a fish in water or a hawk on the wing. Otherwise he could have been any gray-haired man of fifty-odd. Neither of them had bothered to put insignia of rank on the coveralls that were standard shipboard working attire.

'Good day,' he said. 'I trust you had a pleasant leave.'

'I certainly did.' The color mounted in her cheeks. 'And you?'

'Oh . . . it was all right. Mostly I played tourist, from end to end of Earth. I was surprised at how much I had not seen before.'

Lindgren regarded him with some compassion. He floated alone by his command seat, one of three clustered around a control and communications console at the middle of the circular room. The meters, readout screens, indicators, and other gear that crowded the bulkheads, already blinking and quivering and tracing out scrawls, only emphasized his isolation. Until she came, he had not been listening to anything except the murmur of ventilators or the infrequent click of a relay.

'You have nobody whatsoever left?' she asked.

'Nobody close.' Telander's long features crinkled in a smile. 'Don't forget, as far as the Solar System is concerned, I have almost counted a century. When last I visited my home village in Dalarna, my brother's grandson was the proud father of two adolescents. It was not to be expected that they would consider me a near relative.'

(He was born three years before the first manned expedition departed for Alpha Centauri. He entered kindergarten two years before the first maser messages from it reached Farside Station on Luna. That set the life of an introverted, idealistic child on trajectory. At age twenty-five, an Academy graduate with a notable performance in the interplanetary ships, he was allowed on the first crew for Epsilon Eridani. They returned twenty-nine years later; but because of the time dilation, they had experienced just eleven, including the six spent at the goal planets. The discoveries they had made covered them with glory. The Tau Ceti ship was outfitting when they came back. Telander could be the first officer if he was willing to leave in less than a year. He was. Thirteen years of his own went by before he returned, commander in place of a captain who had died on a world of peculiar savageries. On Earth, the interval had been thirty-one years. *Leonora Christine* was being assembled in orbit. Who better than him for her master? He hesitated. She was to start in barely three years. If he accepted, most of those thousand days would be spent planning and preparing . . . . But not to accept was probably not thinkable; and too, he walked as a stranger on an Earth grown strange to him.)

'Let's get busy,' he said. 'I assume Boris Fedoroff and his engineers rode up with you?'

She nodded. 'You'll hear him on the intercom after he's organized, he told me.'

'Hm. He might have observed the courtesy of notifying me of his arrival.'

'He's in a foul mood. Sulked the whole way from ground. I don't know why. Does it matter?'

'We are going to be together in this hull for quite a while, Ingrid,' Telander remarked. 'Our behavior will indeed matter.'

'Oh, Boris will get over his fit. I suppose he has a hangover, or some girl said no to him last night, or something. He struck me during training as a rather soft-hearted person.'

'The psychoprofile indicates it. Still, there are things – potentialities – in each of us that no testing shows. You have to be yonder – ' Telander gestured at the hood of the optical periscope, as if it were the remoteness that it watched – 'before those develop, for good or bad. And they do. They

20

always do.' He cleared his throat. 'Well. The scientific personnel are on schedule also?'

'Yes. They'll arrive in two ferries, first at 1340 hours, second at 1500.' Telander noted agreement with the program clamped to the desk part of the console. Lindgren added: 'I don't believe we need that much interval between them.'

'Safety margin,' Telander replied absently. 'Besides, training or no, we'll need time to get that many ground-lubbers to their berths, when they can't handle themselves properly in weightlessness.'

'Carl can handle them,' Lindgren said. 'If need be, he can carry them individually, faster than you'd credit till you saw him.'

'Reymont? Our constable?' Telander studied her fluttering lashes. 'I know he's skilled in free fall, and he'll come on the first ferry, but is he that good?'

'We visited L'Etoile de Plaisir.'

'Where?'

'A resort satellite.'

'Hm, yes, that one. And you played null-gee games?' Lindgren nodded, not looking at the captain. He smiled again. 'Among other things, no doubt.'

'He'll be staying with me.'

'Um-m-m....' Telander rubbed his chin. 'To be honest, I'd rather have him in the cabin already agreed on, in case of trouble among the, um, passengers. That's what he's for, en route.'

'I could join him,' Lindgren offered.

Telander shook his head. 'No. Officers must live in officer country. The theoretical reason, having them next to bridge level, isn't the real one. You'll find out how important symbols are, Ingrid, in the next five years.' He shrugged. 'Well, the other cabins are only one deck abaft ours. I daresay he can get to them soon enough if need be. Assuming your arranged room-mate doesn't mind a swap, have your wish, then.'

'Thank you,' she said low.

'I can't help being a little surprised,' Telander confessed.

'He doesn't appear to me as the sort you'd choose. Do you think the relationship will last?'

'I hope it will. He says he wants it to.' She broke from her confusion with a teasing attack: 'What about you? Have you made any commitments yet?'

'No. In time, doubtless, in time. I'll be too busy at first. At my age these matters aren't that urgent.' Telander laughed, then grew earnest. 'A propos time, we've none to waste. Please carry out your inspections and – '

The ferry made rendezvous and docked. Bond anchors extended to hold its stubby hull against the larger curve of *Leonora Christine*. Her robots – sensor-computer-effector units – directing the terminal maneuvers caused airlocks to join in an exact kiss. More than that would be demanded of them later. Both chambers being exhausted, their outer valves swung back, enabling a plastic tube to make an airtight seal. The locks were repressurized and checked for a possible leak. When none was found, the inner valves opened.

Reymont unharnessed himself. Floating free of his seat, he glanced down the length of the passenger section. The American chemist, Norbert Williams, was unbuckling too. 'Hold it,' Reymont commanded in English. While everyone knew Swedish, some did not know it well. For scientists, English and Russian remained the chief international tongues. 'Keep your places. I told you at the port, I'll escort you singly to your cabins.'

'You needn't bother with me,' Williams answered. 'I can get around weightless okay.' He was short, round-faced, sandy-haired, given to colorful garments and to speaking rather loudly.

'You all had some drill in it,' Reymont said. 'But that's not the same thing as getting the right reflexes built in through experience.'

'So we flounder a bit. So what?'

'So an accident is possible. Not probable, I agree, but possible. My duty is to help forestall such possibilities. My judgment is that I should conduct you to your berths, where you will remain until further notice.'

Williams reddened. 'See here, Reymont – '

The constable's eyes, which were gray, turned full upon him. 'That's a direct order,' Reymont said, word by word. 'I have the authority. Let us not begin this voyage with a breach.'

Williams resecured himself. His motions were needlessly energetic, his lips clamped tight together. A few drops of sweat broke off his forehead and bobbed in the aisles; the overhead fluoro made them sparkle.

Reymont spoke by intercom to the pilot. That man would not board the ship, but would boost off as soon as his human cargo was discharged. 'Do you mind if we unshutter? Give your friends something to look at while they wait.'

'Go ahead,' said the voice. 'No hazard indicated. And ... they won't see Earth again for a spell, will they?'

Reymont announced the permission. Hands eagerly turned cranks on the spaceward side of the boat, sliding back the plates that covered the glasyl viewports. Reymont got busy with his shepherding.

Fourth in line was Chi-Yuen Ai-Ling. She had twisted about in her safety webbing to face the port entirely. Her fingers were pressed against its surface. 'Now you, please,' Reymont said. She didn't respond. 'Miss Chi-Yuen.' He tapped her shoulder. 'You're next.'

'Oh!' She might have been shaken out of a dream. Tears stood in her eyes. 'I, I beg your pardon. I was lost – '

The linked spacecraft were coming into another dawn. Light soared over Earth's immense horizon, breaking in a thousand colors from maple-leaf scarlet to peacock blue. Momentarily a wing of zodiacal radiance could be seen, like a halo over the rising fire-disk. Beyond were the stars and a crescent moon. Below was the planet, agleam with her oceans, her clouds where rain and thunder walked, her green-brown-snowy continents and jewel-box cities. You saw, you felt, that this world lived.

Chi-Yuen fumbled with her buckles. Her hands looked too thin for them. 'I hate to stop watching,' she whispered in French. 'Rest well there, Jacques.'

'You'll be free to observe on the ship screens, once we've

23

commenced acceleration,' Reymont told her in the same language.

The fact that he spoke it startled her back to ordinariness. 'Then we will be going away,' she said, but with a smile. Her mood had evidently been more ecstatic than elegiac.

She was small, frail-boned, her figure seeming a boy's in the high-collared tunic and wide-cut slacks of the newest Oriental mode. Men tended to agree, however, that she had the most enchanting face aboard, coifed in shoulder-length blue-black hair. When she spoke Swedish, the trace of Chinese intonation that she gave its natural lilt made it a song.

Reymont helped her unstrap and laid an arm around her waist. He didn't bother with shuffling along in bondsole shoes. Instead, he pushed one foot against the chair and flew down the aisle. At the lock he seized a handhold, swung through an arc, gave himself a fresh shove, and was inside the starship. In general, those whom he escorted relaxed; it was easier for him to carry them passive than to contend with their clumsy efforts to help. But Chi-Yuen was different. She knew how. Their movements turned into a swift, swooping dance. After all, as a planetologist she had had a good deal of experience with free fall.

Their flight was not less exhilarating for being explainable. The companionway from the airlock ran through concentric layers of storage decks: extra shielding and armor for the cylinder at the axis of the ship which housed personnel. Elevators could be operated there, to carry heavy loads forward or aft under acceleration. But probably the stairs which spiraled through wells parallel to the elevator shafts would see more use. Reymont and Chi-Yuen took one of these to get from the center-of-mass deck devoted to electrical and gyroscopic machinery, bow-ward to the living quarters. Weightless, they hauled themselves along the stair rail, never touching a step. At the speed they acquired, centrifugal and Coriolis forces made them somewhat dizzy, like a mild drunkenness bringing forth laughter. 'And ay-round we go ay-gain . . . whee!'

The cabins for those other than officers opened on two corridors which flanked a row of bathrooms. Each compartment was two meters high and four square; it had two doors, two closets, two built-in dressers with shelves above, and two folding beds. These last could be slid together on tracks to form one, or be pushed apart. In the second case, it then became possible to lower a screen from the overhead and thus turn the double room into two singles.

'That was a trip to write about in my diary, Constable.' Chi-Yuen clutched a handhold and leaned her forehead against the cool metal. Mirth still trembled on her mouth.

'Who are you sharing this with?' Reymont asked.

'For the present, Jane Sadler.' Chi-Yuen opened her eyes and let them glint at him. 'Unless you have a different idea?'

'Heh? Uh . . . I'm with Ingrid Lindgren.'

'Already?' The mood dropped from her. 'Forgive me. I should not pry.'

'No, I'm the one who owes the apology,' he said. 'Making you wait here with nothing to do, as if you couldn't manage in free fall.'

'You can't make exceptions.' Chi-Yuen was altogether serious again. She extended her bed, floated onto it, and started harnessing in. 'I want to lie awhile alone anyway and think.'

'About Earth?'

'About many things. We are leaving more than most of us have yet understood, Charles Reymont. It is a kind of death – followed by resurrection, perhaps, but nonetheless a death.'

CHAPTER 3

' – zero!'

The ion drive came to life. No man could have gone behind its thick shielding to watch it and survived. Nor could he listen to it, or feel any vibration of its power. It was too efficient for that. In the so-called engine room, which was actually an electronic nerve center, men did hear the faint throb of pumps feeding reaction mass from the tanks. They hardly noticed, being intent on the meters, displays, readouts, and code signals which monitored the system. Boris Fedoroff's hand was never distant from the primary cutoff switch. Between him and Captain Telander in the command bridge flowed a mutter of observations. It was not necessary to *Leonora Christine*. Far less sophisticated craft than she could operate themselves. And she was in fact doing so. Her intermeshing built-in robots worked with more speed and precision – more flexibility, even, within the limits of their programming – than mortal flesh could hope for. But to stand by was a necessity for the men themselves.

Elsewhere, the sole direct proof of motion that those had who lay in their cabins was a return of weight. It was not much, under one tenth gee, but it gave them an 'up' and 'down' for which their bodies were grateful. They released themselves from their beds. Reymont announced over the hall intercom: 'Constable to personnel off watch. You may move around *ad libitum* – forward of your deck, that is.' Sarcastically: 'You may recall that an official good-by ceremony, complete with benediction, will be broadcast at Greenwich noon. We'll screen it in the gymnasium for those who care to watch.'

Reaction mass entered the fire chamber. Thermonuclear generators energized the furious electric arcs that stripped those atoms down to ions; the magnetic fields that separated positive and negative particles; the forces that focused them into beams; the pulses that lashed them to ever higher velocities as they sped down the rings of the thrust tubes, until they emerged scarcely less fast than light itself. Their blast was invisible. No energy was wasted on flames. Instead, everything that the laws of physics permitted was spent on driving *Leonora Christine* outward.

A vessel her size could not accelerate by this means like a Patrol cruiser. That would have demanded more fuel than she could hold, who must carry half a hundred people, and their necessities for ten or fifteen years, and their tools for satisfying scientific curiosity after they arrived, and (if the data beamed by the instrumented probe which had preceded her did actually mean that the third planet of Beta Virginis was habitable) the supplies and machines whereby man could begin to take a new world for himself. She spiraled slowly out of Earth orbit. The dwellers within her had ample chances to stand at her view-screens and watch home dwindle among the stars.

There was no space to spare in space. Every cubic centimeter inside the hull must work. Yet persons intelligent and sensitive enough to adventure out here would have gone crazy in a 'functional' environment. Thus far the bulkheads were bare metal and plastic. But the artistically talented had plans. Reymont noticed Emma Glassgold, molecular biologist, in a corridor, sketching out a mural that would show forest around a sunlit lake. And from the start, the residential and recreational decks were covered with a material green and springy as grass. The air gusting from the ventilators was more than purified by the plants of the hydroponic section and the colloids of the Darrell balancer. It went through changes of temperature, ionization, odor. At present it smelled like fresh clover – with an appetizing whiff added if you passed the galley, since gourmet food compensates for many deprivations.

Similarly, commons was a warren occupying a whole deck. The gymnasium, which doubled as theater and assembly room, was its largest unit. But even the mess was of a size to let diners stretch their legs and relax. Nearby were hobby shops, a clubroom for sedentary games, a swimming pool, tiny gardens and bowers. Some of the ship's designers had argued against putting the dream boxes on this level. Should folk come here for fun be reminded by the door of that cabin that they must have ghostly substitutes for the realities they had left behind them? But the process was, after all, a sort of recreation too; having it in sick bay might be unpleasant, and that was the sole alternative.

There was no immediate need for that apparatus. The journey was still young. A slightly hysterical gaiety filled the atmosphere. Men roughhoused, women chattered, laughter was inordinate at mealtimes, and the frequent dances were occasions of heavy flirtation. Passing the gym, which stood open, Reymont saw a handball match in progress. At low gee, when you could virtually walk up a wall, the action got spectacular.

He continued to the pool. In an alcove off the principal corridor, it could hold several without crowding; but at this hour, 2100, no one was using it. Jane Sadler stood at the edge, frowning thoughtfully. She was a Canadian, a bio-technician in the organocycle department. Physically she was a big brunette, her features ordinary but the rest of her shown to high advantage by shorts and tee shirt.

'Troubles?' Reymont asked.

'Oh, hullo, Constable,' she responded in English. 'Nothing wrong, except I can't figure out how best to decorate in here. I'm supposed to make recommendations to my committee.'

'Didn't they plan on a Roman bath effect?'

'Uh-huh. That covers a lot of ground, though. Nymphs and satyrs, or poplar groves, or temple buildings, or what?' She laughed. 'Hell with it. I'll suggest N & S. If the job gets botched, it can always be done over, till we run out of paint. Give us something further to do.'

'Who can keep going five years – and five more, if we have to return – on hobbies?' Reymont said slowly.

Sadler laughed again. 'Nobody. Don't fret. Everyone aboard has a full program of work lined up, whether it be theoretical research or writing the Great Space Age Novel or teaching Greek in exchange for tensor calculus.'

'Of course. I've seen the proposals. Are they adequate?'

'Constable, do relax! The other expeditions made it, more or less sanely. Why not us? Take your swim.' She grinned wider. 'While you're at it, soak your head.'

Reymont imitated a smile, removed his clothes, and hung them on a rack. She whistled. 'Hey,' she said, 'I hadn't seen you before in less'n a coverall. That's some collection of biceps and triceps and things you pack around. Calis-thenics?'

'In my job, I'd better keep fit,' he replied uncomfortably.

'Some offwatch when you've nothing else to do,' she suggested, 'come around to my cabin and exercise me.'

'I'd enjoy that,' he said, looking her up and down, 'but at present Ingrid and I – '

'Yeah, sure. I was kidding, sort of, anyway. Seems like I'll be making a steady liaison soon myself.'

'Really? Who, if I may ask?'

'Elof Nilsson.' She lifted a hand. 'No, don't say it. He's not exactly Adonis. His manners aren't always the sweetest. But he's got a wonderful mind, the best in the ship, I suspect. You don't get bored listening to him.' Her gaze shifted aside. 'He's pretty lonely too.'

Reymont stood quiet for a moment. 'And you're pretty fine, Jane,' he said. 'Ingrid's meeting me here. Why don't you join us?'

She cocked her head. 'By golly, you do keep a human being hidden under that policeman. Don't worry, I won't let out your secret. And I won't stay, either. Privacy's hard to come by. You two use this while you've got it.'

She waved and left. Reymont peered after her and back down into the water. He was standing thus when Lindgren arrived.

'Sorry I'm late,' she said. 'Beamcast from Luna. Another idiotic inquiry about how things are going for us. I'll be positively glad when we get out into the Big Deep.' She kissed him. He hardly responded. She stepped back, trouble clouding her face. 'What's the matter, darling?'

'Do you think I'm too stiff?' he blurted.

She had no instant reply. The fluorolight gleamed on her tawny hair, a ventilator's breeze ruffled it a little, the noise of the ball game drifted through the entrance arch. Finally: 'What makes you wonder?'

'A remark. Well meant, but a slight shock just the same.'

Lindgren frowned. 'I've told you before, you've been heavier-handed than I quite liked, the few times you've had to make somebody toe the line. No one aboard is a fool, a malingerer, or a saboteur.'

'Should I not have told Norbert Williams to shut up the

other day, when he started denouncing Sweden at mess? Things like that can have a rather nasty end result.' Reymont laid a clenched fist in the other palm. 'I know,' he said. 'Military-type discipline isn't needed, isn't desirable . . . yet. But I've seen so much death, Ingrid. The time could come when we won't survive, unless we can act as one and jump to a command.'

'Well, conceivably on Beta Three,' Lindgren admitted. 'Though the robot didn't send any data suggesting intelligent life. At most, we might encounter savages armed with spears – who would probably not be hostile to us.'

'I was thinking of hazards like storms, landslips, diseases, God knows what on an entire world that isn't Earth. Or a disaster before we get there. I'm not convinced modern man knows everything about the universe.'

'We've covered this ground too often.'

'Yes. It's old as space flight; older. That doesn't make it less real.' Reymont groped for sentences. 'What I'm trying to do is – I'm not sure. This situation is not like any other I was ever in. I'm trying to . . . . somehow . . . keep alive some idea of authority. Beyond simple obedience to the articles and the officers. Authority which has the right to command anything, to command a man to death, if that's needful for saving the rest – ' He stared into her puzzlement. 'No,' he sighed, 'you don't understand. You can't. Your world was always good.'

'Maybe you can explain it to me, if you say it enough different ways.' She spoke softly. 'And maybe I can make a few things clear to you. It won't be easy. You've never taken off your armor, Carl. But we'll try, shall we?' She smiled and slapped the hardness of his thigh. 'Right now, though, silly, we're supposed to be off duty. What about that swim?'

She slipped out of her garments. He watched her approach him. She liked strenuous sports and lying under a sun lamp afterward. It showed in full breasts and hips, slim waist, long supple limbs, a tan against which her blondness stood vivid. '*Bozhe moi*, you're beautiful!' he said low in his throat.

30

She pirouetted. 'At your service, kind sir – if you can catch me!' She made four low-gravity leaps to the end of the diving board and plunged cleanly off it. Her descent was dreamlike slow, a chance for aerial ballet. The splash when she struck made lingering lacy patterns.

Reymont entered directly from the poolside. Swimming was hardly different under this acceleration. The thrust of muscles, the cool silken flowing of water, would be the same at the galaxy's rim, and beyond. Ingrid Lindgren had said once that such truths made her doubt she would ever become really homesick. Man's house was the whole cosmos.

Tonight she frolicked, ducking, dodging, slipping from his grasp again and again. Their laughter echoed between the walls. When at last he cornered her, she embraced his neck in turn, laid her lips to his ear and whispered: 'Well, you did catch me.'

'M-m-m-hm.' Reymont kissed the hollow between shoulder and throat. Through the wetness he smelled live girlflesh. 'Grab our clothes and we'll go.'

He carried her six kilos easily on one arm. When they were alone in the stairwell, he caressed her with his free hand. She kicked her heels and giggled. 'Sensualist!'

'We'll soon be back under a whole gee,' he reminded her, and started bounding down to officer level at a speed that would have broken necks on Earth.

– Later she raised herself on an elbow and met his eyes with hers. She had set the lights dim. Shadows moved behind her, around her, making her doubly gold- and amber-hued. With a finger she traced his profile.

'You're a wonderful lover, Carl,' she murmured. 'I've never had a better.'

'I'm fond of you too,' he said.

A hint of pain touched brow and voice. 'But that's the only time you really give of yourself. And do you, altogether, even then?'

'What is there to give?' His tone roughened. 'I've told you about things that happened to me in the past.'

'Anecdotes. Episodes. No connection, no – There at the pool, for the first time, you offered me a glimpse of what you are. The tiniest possible glimpse, and you hid it away at once. Why? I wouldn't use the insight to hurt you, Carl.'

He sat up, scowling. 'I don't know what you mean. People learn about each other, living together. You know I admire classical artists like Rembrandt and Bonestell, and don't care for abstractions or chromodynamics. I'm not very musical. I have a barrack-room sense of humour. My politics are conservative. I prefer tournedos to filet mignon but wish the culture tanks could supply us with either more often. I play a wicked game of poker, or would if there were any point in it aboard this ship. I enjoy working with my hands and am good at it, so I'll be helping build the laboratory facilities once that project gets organized. I'm currently trying to read *War and Peace* but keep falling asleep.' He smote the mattress. 'What more do you need?'

'Everything,' she answered sadly. She gestured around the room. Her closet happened to stand open, revealing the innocent vanity of her best gowns. The shelves were filled with her private treasures, to the limit of her mass allowance – a battered old copy of Bellman, a lute, a dozen pictures waiting their turn to be hung, smaller portraits of her kinfolk, a Hopi kachina doll . . . 'You brought nothing personal.'

'I've traveled light through life.'

'On a hard road, I think. Maybe someday you'll dare trust me.' She drew close to him. 'Never mind now, Carl. I don't want to harass you. I want you in me again. You see, this has stopped being a matter of friendship and convenience. I've fallen in love with you.'

When the appropriate speed was reached, lining out of Earth's domain toward that sign of the zodiac where the Virgin ruled, *Leonora Christine* went free. Thrusters cold, she became another comet. Gravitation alone worked upon her, bending her path, diminishing her haste.

It had been allowed for. But the effect must be kept minimal. The uncertainties of interstellar navigation were too large as was, without adding an extra factor. So the crew – the professional spacemen, as distinguished from the

32

scientific and technical personnel – worked under a time limit.

Boris Fedoroff led a gang outside. Their job was tricky. You needed skill to labor in weightlessness and not exhaust yourself trying to control tools and body. The best of men could still let both bondsoles lose their grip on the ship frame. You would float off, cursing, nauseated by spin forces, until you brought up at the end of your lifeline and hauled yourself back. Lighting was poor: unshielded glare in the sun, ink blackness in shadow except for what puddles of undiffused radiance were cast by helmet lamps. Hearing was no better. Words had trouble getting through the sounds of harsh breath and thuttering blood, when these were confined in a spacesuit, and through the cosmic seething in radio earplugs. For lack of air purification comparable to the ship's, gaseous wastes were imperfectly removed. They accumulated over hours until you toiled in a haze of sweat smell, water vapor, carbon dioxide, hydrogen sulfide, acetone . . . and your undergarments clung sodden to your skin . . . and you looked wearily through your face-place at the stars, with a band of headache behind your eyes.

Nevertheless, the Bussard module, the hilt and pommel of the dagger, was detached. Maneuvering it away from the vessel was tough, dangerous labor. Without friction or weight, it kept every gram of its considerable inertial mass. It was as hard to stop as to set in motion.

Finally it trailed aft on a cable. Fedoroff checked the positioning himself. 'Done,' he grunted. 'I hope.' His men clipped their lifelines to the cable. He did likewise, spoke to Telander in the bridge, and cast off. The cable was reeled back inboard, taking the engineers along.

They had need for haste. While the module would follow the hull on more or less the same orbit, differential influences were acting. They would soon cause an undesirable shift in relative alignments. But everyone must be inside before the next stage of the process. The forces about to be established would not be kind to living organisms.

Leonora Christine extended her scoopfield webs. They glistened in the sunlight, silver across starry black. From afar she might have suggested a spider, one of those adventurous little arachnids that went flying off with kites made of dewy silk. She was not, after all, anything big or important in the universe.

Yet what she did was awesome enough on the human scale. Her interior power plant sent energy coursing into the scoopfield generators. From their controlling webwork sprang a field of magnetohydrodynamic forces – invisible but reaching across thousands of kilometres; a dynamic interplay, not a static configuration, but maintained and adjusted with nigh absolute precision; enormously strong but even more enormously complex.

The forces seized the trailing Bussard unit, brought it into micrometrically exact position with respect to the hull, locked it in place. Monitors verified that everything was in order. Captain Telander made a final check with the Patrol on Luna, received his go-ahead, and issued a command. From then on, the robots took over.

Low acceleration on ion thrust had built up a modest outward speed, measurable in tens of kilometers per second. It sufficed to start the star-drive engine. The power available increased by orders of magnitude. At a full one gravity, *Leonora Christine* began to move!

CHAPTER 4

In one of the garden rooms stood a viewscreen tuned to Outside. Sable and diamonds were startlingly framed by ferns, orchids, overarching fuchsia and bougainvillea. A fountain tinkled and glittered. The air was warmer here than in most places aboard, moist, full of perfumes and greenness.

None of it quite did away with the underlying pulse of driving energies. Bussard systems had not been developed to the smoothness of electric rockets. Always, now, the ship whispered and shivered. The vibration was faint, on the very edge of awareness, but it wove its way through metal, bones, and maybe dreams.

Emma Glassgold and Chi-Yuen Ai-Ling sat on a bench among the flowers. They had been walking about, feeling their way toward friendship. Since entering the garden, however, they had fallen silent.

Abruptly Glassgold winced and pulled her vision from the screen. 'It was a mistake to come here,' she said. 'Let us go.'

'Why, I find it charming,' the planetologist answered, surprised. 'An escape from bare walls that we'll need years to make sightly.'

'No escape from that.' Glassgold pointed at the screen. It happened at the moment to be scanning aft and so held an image of the sun, shrunken to the brightest of the stars.

Chi-Yuen regarded her narrowly. The molecular biologist was likewise small and dark-haired, but her eyes were round and blue, her face round and pink, her body a trifle on the dumpy side. She dressed plainly whether working or not; and without snubbing social activities, she had hitherto been observer rather than participant.

'In – how long? – a couple of weeks,' she continued, 'we have reached the marches of the Solar System. Every day – no, every twenty-four hours; "day" and "night" mean nothing any longer – each twenty-four hours we gain 845 kilometers per second in speed.'

'A shrimp like me is grateful to have full Earth weight,' Chi-Yuen said with attempted lightness.

'Don't misunderstand me,' Glassgold replied hastily. 'I won't scream, "Turn back! Turn back!" ' She tried a joke of her own. 'That would be too disappointing to the psychologists who checked me out.' The joke dissipated. 'It is only . . . I find I require time . . . to get used, piece by piece, to this.'

Chi-Yuen nodded. She, in her newest and most colorful cheong-sam – among her hobbies was making over her clothes – could almost have belonged to a different species from Glassgold. But she patted the other woman's hand and said: 'You are not unique, Emma. It was expected. People begin to realize with more than brains, in their whole beings, what it means to be on such a voyage.'

'You don't seem bothered.'

'No. Not since Earth disappeared in the sun glare. And not unbearably before. It hurt to say good-by. But I've had experience in that. One learns how to look forward.'

'I am ashamed,' Glassgold said. 'When I have had so much more than you. Or has that made me soft in the spirit?'

'Have you really?' Chi-Yuen's question was muted.

'Why . . . yes. Haven't I? Or don't you recall? My parents were always well-to-do. Father is an engineer in a desalinization plant, Mother an agronomist. The Negev is beautiful when the crops are growing, and calm, friendly, not hectic like Tel Aviv or Haifa. Though I did enjoy studying at the university. I had chances to travel, with good companions. My work went fine. Yes, I was lucky.'

'Then why did you enlist for Beta Three?'

'Scientific interest . . . a whole new planetary evolution –'

'No, Emma.' The raven's wing tresses stirred as Chi-Yuen shook her head. 'The earlier starships brought back data to keep research going for a hundred years, right on Earth. What are you running from?'

Glassgold bit her lip. 'I shouldn't have pried,' Chi-Yuen apologized. 'I was hoping to help.'

'I will tell you,' Glassgold said. 'I have a feeling you might indeed help. You are younger than me, but you have seen more.' Her fingers knitted together in her lap. 'I'm not quite sure, though, myself. How did the cities begin to seem vulgar and empty? And when I went home to visit my people, the countryside seemed smug and empty. I thought I might find . . . a purpose? . . . out here. I don't know. I applied for the berth on impulse. When I was called for serious testing, my parents made a fuss till I could not back down. And yet we were always a close family. It was such a pain leaving them. My big, confident father, he was suddenly little and old.'

'Was a man involved too?' Chi-Yuen asked. 'I'll tell you, because it's no secret – he and I were engaged, and everything about this crew that was ever on public record went into the dossiers – there was for me.'

'A fellow student,' Glassgold said humbly. 'I loved him. I still do. He hardly knew I existed.'

'Not uncommon,' Chi-Yuen answered. 'One gets over it, or else turns it into a sickness. You're healthy in the head, Emma. What you need is to come out of your shell. Mix with your shipmates. Care about them. Get out of your cabin for a while and into a man's.'

Glassgold flushed. 'I don't hold with those practices.'

Chi-Yuen's brows lifted. 'Are you a virgin? We can't afford that, if we're to start a new race on Beta Three. The genetic material is scarce at best.'

'I want a decent marriage,' Glassgold said with a flick of anger, 'and as many children as God gives me. But they will know who their father is. It doesn't hurt if I don't play any ridiculous game of musical beds while we travel. We have enough girls aboard who do.'

'Like me.' Chi-Yuen was unruffled. 'No doubt stable relationships will evolve. Meanwhile, now and then, why not give and get a few moments of pleasure?'

'I'm sorry,' Glassgold said. 'I shouldn't criticize private matters. Especially when lives have been as different as yours and mine.'

'True. I don't agree that mine was less fortunate than yours. On the contrary.'

'What?' Glassgold's mouth fell open. 'You can't be serious!'

Chi-Yuen smiled. 'You have only learned the surface of my past, Emma, if that. I can guess what you're thinking. My country divided, impoverished, spastic from the aftermath of revolutions and civil wars. My family cultured and tradition-minded but poor with the desperate poverty that none except aristocrats fallen on evil times know. Their sacrifices to keep me in the Sorbonne, when the chance came. After I got my degree, the hard work and sacrifice I made in return, helping them get back on their feet.' She turned her face to the ebbing light of Sol and added most quietly: 'About my man. We, too, were students together, in Paris. Later, as I said, I must often be away from him because of work. Finally he went to visit my parents in Peking. I was to join him as soon as possible, and we would be married, in law and sacrament as well as in fact. A riot happened. He was killed.'

'Oh, my dear – ' Glassgold began.

'That's the surface,' Chi-Yuen interrupted. 'The surface. Don't you see, I also had a loving home, perhaps more than you did, because at the end they understood me so well that they didn't resist my leaving them forever. I saw a lot of the world, more than can be seen traveling carefully by first class. I *had* my Jacques. And others, before, afterward, as he would have wanted. I'm outward bound with no regrets and no pain that won't heal. The luck is mine, Emma.'

Glassgold did not respond with words.

Chi-Yuen took her by the hand and stood up. 'You must break free of yourself,' the planetologist said. 'In the long run, only you can teach you how to do that. But maybe I can help a little. Come down to my cabin. We'll make you a gown that does you justice. The Covenant Day party will be soon, and I intend for you to have fun.'

Consider: a single light-year is an inconceivable abyss. Denumerable but inconceivable. At an ordinary speed – say, a reasonable pace for a car in megalopolitan traffic, two kilometers per minute – you would consume almost nine million years in crossing it. And in Sol's neighborhood, the stars averaged some nine light-years apart. Beta Virginis was thirty-two distant.

Nevertheless, such spaces could be conquered. A ship accelerating continuously at one gravity would have traveled half a light-year in slightly less than one year of time. And she would be moving very near the ultimate velocity, three hundred thousand kilometers per second.

Practical problems arose. Where was the mass-energy to do this coming from? Even in a Newtonian universe, the thought of a rocket, carrying that much fuel along from the start, would be ludicrous. Still more so was it in the true, Einsteinian cosmos, where the mass of ship and payload increased with speed, climbing toward infinity as that speed approached light's.

But fuel and reaction mass were there in space! It was pervaded with hydrogen. Granted, the concentration was not great by terrestrial standards: about one atom per cubic centimeter in the galactic vicinity of Sol. Nevertheless, this made thirty billion atoms per second, striking every square centimeter of the ship's cross section, when she approximated light velocity. (The figure was comparable at earlier stages of her voyage, since the interstellar medium was denser close to a star.) The energies were appalling. Megaroentgens of hard radiation would be released by impact; and less than a thousand r within an hour are fatal. No material shielding would help. Even supposing it impossibly thick to start with, it would soon be eroded away.

However, in the days of *Leonora Christine* non-material means were available: magnetohydrodynamic fields, whose pulses reached forth across millions of kilometers to seize atoms by their dipoles – no need for ionization – and control their streaming. These fields did not serve passively, as mere armor. They deflected dust, yes, and all gases except the dominant hydrogen. But this latter was forced aft – in long curves that avoided the hull by a safe margin – until it entered a vortex of compressing, kindling electromagnetism centered on the Bussard engine.

The ship was not small. Yet she was the barest glint of metal in that vast web of forces which surrounded her. She herself no longer generated them. She had initiated the process when she attained minimum ramjet speed; but it became too huge, too swift, until it could only be created and sustained by itself. The primary thermonuclear reactors (a separate system would be used to decelerate), the venturi tubes, the entire complex which thrust her was not contained inboard. Most of it was not material at all, but a resultant of cosmic-scale vectors. The ship's control devices, under computer direction, were not remotely analogous to autopilots. They were like catalysts which, judiciously used, could affect the course of those monstrous reactions, could build them up, in time slow them down and snuff them out . . . but not fast.

Starlike burned the hydrogen fusion, aft of the Bussard module that focused the electromagnetism which contained it. A titanic gas-laser effect aimed photons themselves in a beam whose reaction pushed the ship forward – and which would have vaporized any solid body it struck. The process was not 100 per cent efficient. But most of the stray energy went to ionize the hydrogen which escaped nuclear combustion. These protons and electrons, together with the fusion products, were also hurled backward by the force fields, a gale of plasma adding its own increment of momentum.

The process was not steady. Rather, it shared the instability of living metabolism and danced always on the same edge of disaster. Unpredictable variations occurred in the matter content of space. The extent, intensity, and configuration of the force fields must be adjusted accordingly – a problem in ? million factors which only a computer could solve fast enough. Incoming data and outgoing signals traveled at light speed: finite speed, requiring a whole three and a third seconds to cross a million kilometers. Response could be fatally slow. This danger would increase as *Leonora Christine* got so close to ultimate velocity that time rates began measurably changing.

Nonetheless, week by week, month by month, she moved on outward.

The multiple cyclings of matter that turned biological wastes back into breathable air, potable water, edible food, usable fiber, went so far as to maintain an equilibrium in the ethyl alcohol aboard. Wine and beer were produced in moderation, mainly for the table. The hard liquor ration was meager. But certain people had included bottles in their personal baggage. Furthermore, they could trade for the share of abstemious friends and save their own issue until it sufficed for a special occasion.

No official rule, but evolving custom, said that drinking outside the cabins took place in the mess. To promote sociability, this room held several small tables rather than a single long one. Hence, between meals, it could double as a club. Some of the men built a bar at one end to dispense ice and mixers. Others made roll-down curtains for the bulkheads, so that the decorous murals could be hidden during boozing hours behind scenes a little more ribald. A taper generally kept background music going, cheerful stuff, anything from sixteenth-century galliards to the latest asteroid ramble received from Earth.

On a particular date at about 2000 hours, the club stood empty. A dance was scheduled in the gym. Most off-duty personnel who wished to attend it – the majority – were getting dressed. Garments, all ceremony, were becoming terribly important. Machinist Johann Freiwald shone in a gilt tunic and silvercloth trews that a lady had made for him. She wasn't ready yet, nor was the orchestra, so he allowed Elof Nilsson to lead him to the bar.

'Can we not talk business tomorrow, though?' he asked. He was a large, amiable young man, square-featured, his scalp shining pink through close-cropped blond hair.

'I want to discuss this with you at once, while it's new in my mind,' said Nilsson's raspy voice. 'It came to me in a flash as I was changing clothes.' His appearance bore him out. 'Before carrying my thought further, I wish to check the practicality.'

'*Jawohl*, if you're supplying the drink and we can keep it short.'

The astronomer found his personal bottle on the shelf, picked up a couple of glasses, and started for a table. 'I take water – ' Freiwald began. The other man didn't hear. 'That's Nilsson for you,' Freiwald told the overhead. He tapped a pitcherful and brought it along.

Nilsson sat down, got out a note pad, and started sketching. He was short, fat, grizzled, and ugly. It was known that an intellectually ambitious father, in the ancient university town Uppsala, had forced him to become a prodigy at the expense of everything else. It was surmised that his marriage had been the result of mutual desperation and had turned into a prolonged catastrophe, for despite a child it dissolved the moment he got a chance to go on this ship. Yet when he talked, not about the humanities he failed to understand and hence disdained, but about his own subject . . . then you forgot his arrogance and flatulence, you remembered his observations which had finally proven the oscillating universe, and you saw him crowned with stars.

' – unparalleled opportunity to get some worthwhile readings. Only think what a baseline we'll have: ten parsecs. Plus the ability to examine gamma-ray spectra with less uncertainty, higher precision, when they're red-shifted down to less energetic photons. And more and more. Still, I'm not satisfied.

'I don't believe it's really necessary for me to peer at an electronic image of the sky – narrow, blurred, and degraded by noise, not to mention the damned optical changes. We should mount mirrors outside the hull. The images they catch could be led along light conductors to eyepieces, photomultipliers, cameras inboard.

'No, don't say it. I'm well aware that previous attempts to do this failed. One could build a machine to go out through an airlock, shape the plastic backing for such an instrument, and aluminize it. But induction effects of the Bussard fields would promptly make the mirror into something appropriate for a fun house in Gröna Lund. Yes.

'Now my idea is to print sensor and feedback circuits into the plastic, controlling flexors that'll automatically compensate these distortions as they occur. I would like your opinion as to the feasibility of designing, testing, and producing those flexors, Mr Freiwald. Here, this is a rough drawing of what I have in mind – '

Nilsson was interrupted. 'Hey, there you are, ol' buddy!' He and the machinist looked up. Williams lurched toward them. The chemist held a bottle in his right hand, a half-full tumbler in the left. His face was redder than usual and he breathed heavily.

'*Was zum Teufel?*' Freiwald exclaimed.

'English, boy,' Williams said. 'Talk English tonight. 'Merican style.' He reached the table, set his burdens down, and rested on it so hard it almost tipped over. A powerful whisky smell hung around him. 'You 'specially, Nilsson.' He pointed with an oscillant finger. 'You talk American tonight, you Swede. Hear me?'

'Please go elsewhere,' the astronomer said.

Williams plumped himself onto a chair. He leaned forward on both elbows. 'You don't know what day this is,' he said. 'Do you?'

'I doubt you do, in your present condition,' Nilsson snapped, remaining with Swedish. 'The date is the fourth of July.'

'R-r-r-right! Y' know what 'at means? No?' Williams turned to Freiwald. 'You know, Heinie?'

'An, uh, anniversary?' the machinist ventured.

'Right. Anniversary. How'd yuh guess?' Williams lifted his glass. 'Drink wi' me, you two. Been collectin' f' today. Drink!'

Freiwald gave him a sympathetic glance and clinked rims. '*Prosit.*' Nilsson started to say, '*Skål,*' but set his own liquor down again and glared.

'Fourth July,' Williams said. 'Independence Day. My country. Wanted throw party. Nobody cared. One drink with me, two maybe, then gotta go their goddam dance.' He regarded Nilsson for a while. 'Swede,' he declared slowly, 'you'll drink wi' me 'r I'll bust y'r teeth in.'

Freiwald laid a muscular hand on Williams' arm. The chemist tried to rise. Freiwald held him where he was. 'Be calm, please, Dr Williams,' the machinist requested mildly. 'If you want to celebrate your national day, why, we'll be glad to toast it. Won't we, sir?' he added to Nilsson.

The astronomer clipped: 'I know what the matter is. I was told before we left, by a man who knew. Frustration. He couldn't cope with modern management procedures.'

'Goddam welfare state bureaucracy,' Williams hiccuped.

'He started dreaming of his country's sovereign, imperial era,' Nilsson went on. 'He fantasized about a free enterprise system that I doubt ever existed. He dabbled in reactionary politics. When the Control Authority had to arrest several high American officials on charges of conspiracy to violate the Covenant –'

'I'd had a bellyful.' Williams' tone rose toward a shout. ' 'Nother star. New world. Chance t' be free. Even if I do have to travel with a pack o' Swedes.'

'You see?' Nilsson grinned at Freiwald. 'He's nothing but a victim of the romantic nationalism that our too orderly world has been consoling itself with, this past generation. Pity he couldn't be satisfied with historical fiction and bad epic poetry.'

'Romantic!' Williams yelled. He struggled fruitlessly in Freiwald's grip. 'You pot-gutted spindle-shanked owl-eyed freak, wha'd'you think it did to you? How'd it feel, being built like that, when the other kids were playing Viking? Your marriage washed out worse'n mine! And I did cope, you son of a bitch, I was meet'n' my payroll, something you never had to do, you – Lemme go an' we'll see who's a man here!'

'Please,' Freiwald said. '*Bitte*. Gentlemen.' He was standing, now, to keep Williams held in the chair. His gaze nailed Nilsson across the table. 'And you, sir,' he continued sharply. 'You had no right to bait him. You might have shown the courtesy to toast his national day.'

Nilsson seemed about to pull intellectual rank. He broke off when Jane Sadler appeared. She had been in the door for a couple of minutes, watching. Her expression made her formal gown pathetic.

'Johann's telling you truth, Elof,' she said. 'Better come along.'

'And dance?' Nilsson gobbled. 'After this?'

'Especially after this.' She tossed her head. 'I've grown pretty tired of you on your high horse, dear. Shall we try to start fresh, or drop everything as of now?'

Nilsson muttered but rose and offered her his arm. She was a little taller than he. Williams sat slumped, struggling not to weep.

'I'll stay here awhile, Jane, and see if I can't cheer him up,' Freiwald whispered to her.

She gave him a troubled smile. 'You would, Johann.' They had been together a few times before she took up with Nilsson. 'Thanks.' Their glances lingered, each on each. Nilsson shuffled his feet and coughed. 'I'll see you later,' she said, and left.

CHAPTER 5

When *Leonora Christine* attained a substantial fraction of light speed, its optical effects became clear to the unaided sight. Her velocity and that of the rays from a star added vectorially; the result was aberration. Except for whatever lay dead aft or ahead, the apparent position changed. Constellations grew lopsided, grew grotesque, and melted, as their members crawled across the dark. More and more, the stars thinned out behind the ship and crowded before her.

Doppler effect operated simultaneously. Because she was fleeing the light waves that overtook her from astern, to her their length was increased and their frequency lowered. In like manner, the waves into which her bow plunged were shortened and quickened. Thus, the sums aft looked ever redder, those forward bluer.

On the bridge stood a compensating viewscope: the single one aboard, elaborate as it was. A computer figured out continuously how the sky would appear if you were motionless at this point in space, and projected a simulacrum of it. The device was not for amusement or comfort; it was a valuable navigational aid.

Clearly, though, the computer needed data on where the ship really was and how fast she was traveling with respect to objects in heaven. This was no simple thing to find out. Velocity – exact speed, exact direction – varied with variations in the interstellar medium and with the necessarily imperfect feedback to the Bussard controls, as well as with time under acceleration. The shifts from her calculated path were comparatively petty; but over astronomical distances, any imprecisions could add up to a fatal sum. They must be eliminated as they occurred.

Hence that neat, stocky, dark-bearded man, Navigation Officer Auguste Boudreau, was among the few who had a full-time job en route that was concerned with operating the ship. It did not quite require him to revolve in a logical circle – find your position and velocity so you can correct for optical phenomena so you can check your position and velocity. Distant galaxies were his primary beacons; statistical analysis of observations made on closer individual stars gave him further data; he used the mathematics of successive approximations.

This made him a collaborator of Captain Telander, who computed and ordered the needful course changes, and of Chief Engineer Fedoroff, who put them into execution. The task was smoothly handled. No one sensed the adjustments, except as an occasional minute temporary increase in the liminal throbbing of the ship, a similarly small and transitory change in the acceleration vector, which felt as if the decks had tilted a few degrees.

In addition, Boudreau and Fedoroff tried to maintain contact with Earth. *Leonora Christine* was still detectable by space-borne instruments in the Solar System. Despite the difficulties created by her drive fields, the Lunar maser beam could still reach her with inquiries, entertainment, news, and personal greetings. She could still reply on her own transmitter. In fact, such talk back and forth was expected to become regular, once she was well established at Beta Virginis. Her unmanned precursor had had no problem with sending information. It was doing so at the present moment, although the ship could not receive that and the crew intended to read its tapes when they arrived.

The present trouble was this: Suns and planets are big, staid objects. They move through space at reasonable speeds, seldom above fifty kilometers per second. And they do not zigzag, however slightly. It is simple to predict where they will be centuries from now, and aim a message beam accordingly. A starship is something else. Men don't last long; they must hurry. Aberration and Doppler shift affect radio too. Eventually the transmissions from Luna would enter on frequencies that nothing aboard the vessel could receive. Well before then, however, through one unforeseeable factor or another, when travel time between maser projector and ship stretched into months, the beam was sure to lose her.

Fedoroff, who was also the communications officer, tinkered with detectors and amplifiers. He strengthened the signals which he punched Solward, hoping they would give clues to his future location. Though days might go by without a break in the silence, he persevered. He was rewarded with success. But the quality of reception was always poorer, the interval of it shorter, the time till the next longer, as *Leonora Christine* entered the Big Deep.

Ingrid Lindgren pushed the buzzer button. The cabins were sufficiently soundproofed that a knock would never pass. There was no response. She tried again, drawing another blank. She hesitated, frowning, shifting from foot to foot. At length she laid hand on catch. The door wasn't locked. She opened it a crack. Not looking through, she called softly, 'Boris. Are you all right?'

Sounds reached her, a creak, a rustle, slow heavy footsteps. Fedoroff threw the door wide. 'Oh,' he said. 'Good day.'

She regarded him. He was a burly man of medium stature, face broad and high in the cheekbones, brown hair salted with gray although his biological age was a mere forty-two. He hadn't shaved for several watches and wore nothing except a robe, obviously thrown on this minute. 'May I come in?' she requested.

'If you wish.' He waved her past him and closed the door. His half of the unit had been screened off from the part currently occupied by Biosystems Chief Pereira. An unmade bed filled most of it. A vodka bottle stood on the dresser.

'Pardon the mess,' he said indifferently. Lumbering past her: 'Would you like a drink? I didn't bring tumblers, but

47

you needn't fear a pull on this. Nobody has anything contagious.' He chuckled, or rather rattled. 'Where would germs come from, here?'

Lindgren sat down on the edge of the bed. 'No, thanks,' she replied. 'I'm on duty.'

'And I'm supposed to be. Yes.' Fedoroff loomed over her, slumping. 'I informed the bridge I feel indisposed and had better take a rest.'

'Shouldn't Dr Latvala examine you?'

'What for? I'm physically well.' Fedoroff paused. 'You came to make sure of me.'

'Part of my job. I'll respect your privacy. But you are a key man.'

Fedoroff smiled. The expression was as forced as the prior noise had been. 'Don't worry,' he said. 'I am not breaking down in the brain either.' He reached for the bottle, then withdrew his arm. 'I am not even glugging myself into a stupor. It is nothing except a . . . what do the Americans call it? . . . a glow.'

'Glows are best in company,' Lindgren declared. After a moment: 'I believe I will accept that drink.'

Fedoroff gave her the bottle and joined her on the bed-side. She raised it to him. '*Skål.*' A scant amount went down her throat. She returned the bottle, and he gave her '*Zdoroviye.*' They sat in silence, Fedoroff gazing at the bulk-head, until he stirred and said:

'Very well. Since you must know. I wouldn't tell anyone else, especially not a woman. But I have come to learn something about you, Ingrid . . . Gunnar's daughter, is that correct?'

'Yes, Boris Ilyitch.'

He gave her a glance and a more nearly genuine smile. She sat relaxed, body curving out her coverall, a hint of warmth and human odor around her. 'I believe – ' his tongue fumbled – 'I hope you will understand, and not repeat what I tell you.'

'I promise the silence. For understanding, I can try.'

He put elbows on knees, hands straining against each others. 'It is personal, you see,' he said slowly and not quite

48

evenly. 'Yet no great matter. I will be over it soon. It is simply . . . that final cast we received . . . upset me.'

'The music?'

'Yes. Music. Signal-to-noise ratio too low for television. Almost too low for sound. The last we will get, Ingrid Gunnar's daughter, before we reach goal and start receiving messages a generation old. I am certain it was the last. Those few minutes, wavering, fading in and out, scarcely to hear through the firecrackle of stars and cosmic rays – when we lost that music, I knew we would get no more.'

Fedoroff's voice trailed off. Lindgren waited.

He shook himself. 'It happened to be a Russian cradle song,' he said. 'My mother sang me to sleep with it.'

She laid a hand on his shoulder and let it rest, feather-light.

'Do not think I am off on an orgy of self-pity,' he added in haste. 'For a short while I remember my dead too well. It will pass.'

'Maybe I do understand,' she murmured.

He was on his second interstellar trip. He had gone to Delta Pavonis. Probe data indicated an Earthlike planet, and the expedition left with flying hopes. The reality was so nightmarish that the survivors showed rare heroism in remaining and studying for the minimum planned time. On their return, they had experienced twelve years; but Earth had aged forty-three.

'I doubt if you do, really.' Fedoroff turned to confront her. 'We expected people would have died when we came home. We expected change. If anything, I was overjoyed at first that I could recognize parts of my city – moonlight on canals and river, domes and towers on Kazan Cathedral, Alexander and Bucephalus rearing over the bridge that carries Nevsky Prospect, the treasures in the Hermitage – ' He looked back away and shook his head wearily. 'But the life itself. That was too different. Meeting it was like, like seeing a woman one loved become a slut.' He fleered. 'Exactly so! I worked in space for five years, as much as I was able, research and development on improving the Bussard engine, as you may remember. My main purpose was to earn the post I have. We can hope for a fresh beginning on Beta Three.'

His words grew barely audible: 'Then my mother's little song reached me. For the last time.' He tilted the bottle to his lips.

Lindgren gave him a minute or two of silence before:

'Now I can see, Boris, in part, why it hurt you so. I've studied a bit of sociohistory. In your boyhood, people were less, well, less relaxed. They'd repaired the war damage in most countries and brought population growth and civil disorder under control. Now they were going on to new things, imagination-staggering projects, on Earth as well as in space. Nothing seemed impossible. At the core of their *élan* was a spirit of hard work, patriotism, dedication. I suppose you had two gods you served with a whole heart, Father Technics and Mother Russia.' Her hand slipped down to lie upon his. 'You returned,' she said, 'and nobody cared.'

He nodded. Teeth caught at his lower lip.

'Is that why you despise today's women?' she asked.

He started. 'No! Never!'

'Why, then, have none of your liaisons lasted beyond a week or two – mostly a single offwatch at a time?' she challenged him. 'Why are you only at ease and merry among men? I believe you don't care to know our half of the human race except as bodies. You don't think there's anything else worth knowing. And what you said a minute ago, about sluts – '

'I came from Delta Pavonis wishing for a true wife,' he answered as if being strangled.

Lindgren sighed. 'Boris, mores change. From my viewpoint, you grew up in a period of unreasonable puritanism. But it was a reaction to an earlier easiness that had perhaps gone too far; and earlier yet – No matter.' She chose her words with care. 'The fact is, man has never stayed by a single ideal. The mass enthusiasm when you were young gave way to cool, rationalistic classicism. Today that's being drowned in turn by a kind of neoromanticism. God knows where that will lead. I probably won't approve.

Regardless, new generations grow up. We've no right to freeze them into our own mold. The universe is too wide.'

Fedoroff was unmoving for so long that she started to rise and go. Suddenly he whirled, caught her wrist, and pulled her back down beside him. His speech labored. 'I would like to know you, Ingrid, as a human being.'

'I'm glad.'

His mouth tightened. 'You had better leave now, though,' he got out. 'You are with Reymont. I don't want to cause trouble.'

'I want you for a friend too, Boris,' she said. 'I've admired you since we first met. Courage, competence, kindliness – what else is there to admire in a man? I wish you could learn to show them to your shipmates that happen to be female.'

He opened his grasp on her. 'I warn you to go.'

She considered him. 'If I do,' she asked, 'and we get to talking another time, will you be at ease with me?'

'I don't know,' he said. 'I hope it, but I don't know.'

She thought awhile further. 'Let us try to make sure of it,' she suggested finally, gently. 'I don't have to be anywhere else for the rest of my watch.'

CHAPTER 6

Every scientist aboard had planned at least one research project to help fill the half decade of travel. Glassgold's was tracing the chemical basis of the life on Epsilon Eridani Two. After setting up her equipment, she began putting her protophytes and tissue cultures through their experimental paces. In due course she got reaction products and needed to know exactly what they were. Norbert Williams was performing analyses for several different people.

One day late in the first year, he brought his report on

her most recent sample to her laboratory. He had taken to doing this in person. The molecules were strange, exciting him as much as her, and the two of them often discussed the findings for hours on end. Increasingly, the conversation would veer toward other topics.

She gave him cheerful greeting as he entered. The workbench behind which she stood was barricaded with test tubes, flasks, a pH meter, a stirrer, a blender, and more. 'Well,' she said, 'I'm quite agog to learn what metabolites my pets have been making now.'

'Damnedest mess I ever saw.' He tossed down a couple of clipped-together pages. 'Sorry, Emma, but you're going to have to run it over. And over and over, I'm afraid. I can't get by with micro quantities. This wants every type of chromatography I've got, plus X-ray diffractions, plus a series of enzyme tests I've listed here, before I'd venture any guess at the structural formulas.'

'I see,' Glassgold replied. 'I regret making more work for you.'

'Shucks, that's what I'm here for, till we reach Beta Three. I'd go nuts without jobs to do, and yours is the most interesting of the lot, I'll tell you.' Williams ran a hand through his hair; the loud shirt wrinkled across his shoulder. 'Though to be frank, I don't understand what's in it for you, other than a pastime. I mean, they're tackling the same problems on Earth, with bigger staff and better facilities. They ought to've cracked your riddles before we come to a stop.'

'No doubt,' she said. 'But will they beam the results to us?'

'I expect not, unless we inquire. And if we do, we'll be very old, or dead, before the reply arrives.' Williams leaned toward her across the bench. 'The thing is, why should we care? Whatever type of biology we find at Beta Three, we know it won't resemble this. Are you keeping your hand in?'

'Partly that,' she admitted. 'I do think it will be of practical value. The broader a view I have of life in the universe, the better I should be able to study the particular case where we are going. And so we learn sooner, more certainly, whether we can build our homes there and call others to follow us from Earth.'

He rubbed his chin. 'Yeah. I guess you're right. Hadn't thought of that angle.'

Awe dwelt beneath the prosaic words. For the expedition was not merely going for a look: not at such cost in resources, labor, skill, dreams, and years. Nor could it hope for anything as easy to subdue as America had been.

At a minimum, these people would spend another half decade in the Beta Virginis System, exploring its worlds in the ship's auxiliary craft, adding what little they could to the little that the orbiting probe had garnered. And if the third planet really was habitable, they would never come home, not even the professional spacemen. They would live out their lives, and belike their children and grandchildren too, exploring its manifold mysteries and flashing their discoveries to the hungry minds on Earth. For indeed, any planet is a *world*, infinitely varied, infinitely secret. And this world appeared to be so terrestroid that the strangenesses it must hold would be yet the more vivid and enlightening.

The folk of *Leonora Christine* were quite explicit in their ambition to establish that kind of scientific base. Their further, largest hope was that their descendants would find no reason ever to go back: that Beta Three might evolve from base to colony to New Earth to jumping-off place for the next starward leap. There was no other way by which men might possess the galaxy.

As if shying away from vistas that could overwhelm her, Glassgold said, reddening a trifle: 'Besides, I care about Eridanian life. It fascinates me. I want to know what . . . makes it tick. And as you point out, if we do stay we aren't likely to get the answers told us while we are alive.'

He fell silent, fiddled with a titration setup, until ship-drive and ventilator breath, sharp chemical odors, bright colors on the reagent and dye shelves, shoved forward into consciousness. At length he cleared his throat. 'Uh, Emma.'

'Yes?' She seemed to feel the same diffidence.

'How about knocking off? Come on down to the club with me for a drink before dinner. My ration.'

She retreated behind her instruments. 'No, thank you,' she said confusedly. 'I, I do have a great deal of work.'

'You have time for it, too,' he pointed out, bolder. 'Okay, if you don't want a cocktail, what about a cup of coffee? Maybe a stroll through the gardens – Look, I don't aim to make a pass. I'd just like to get better acquainted.'

She swallowed before she smiled, but then she gave him warmth. 'Very well, Norbert, I would like that myself.'

A year after she started, *Leonora Christine* was close to her ultimate velocity. It would take her thirty-one years to cross interstellar space, and one year more to decelerate as she approached her target sun.

But that is an incomplete statement. It takes no account of relativity. Precisely because there is an absolute limiting speed (at which light travels *in vacuo*; likewise neutrinos) there is an interdependence of space, time, matter, and energy. The tau factor enters the equations. If v is the (uniform) velocity of a spaceship, and c the velocity of light, then tau equals

$$\sqrt{1 - \frac{v^2}{c^2}}.$$

The closer that v comes to c, the closer tau comes to zero.

Suppose an outside observer measures the mass of the spaceship. The result he gets is her rest mass – i.e., the mass that she has when she is not moving with respect to him – divided by tau. Thus, the faster she travels the more massive she is, as regards the universe at large. She gets the extra mass from the kinetic energy of motion; $e = mc^2$.

Furthermore, if the 'stationary' observer could compare the ship's clocks with his own, he would notice a disagreement. The interlude between two events (such as the birth

54

and death of a man) measured aboard the ship where they take place, is equal to the interlude which the observer measures . . . multiplied by tau. One might say that time moves proportionately slower on a starship.

Lengths shrink; the observer sees the ship shortened in the direction of motion by the factor tau.

Now measurements made on shipboard are every bit as valid as those made elsewhere. To a crewman, looking forth at the universe, the stars are compressed and have gained in mass; the distances between them have shriveled; they shine, they evolve at a strangely reduced rate.

Yet the picture is more complicated even than this. You must bear in mind that the ship has, in fact, been accelerated and will be decelerated in relation to the total background of the cosmos. This takes the whole problem out of special and into general relativity. The star-and-ship situation is not really symmetrical. The twin paradox does not arise. When velocities match once more and reunion takes place, the star will have passed through a longer time than the ship did.

If you ran tau down to one one-hundredth and went into free fall, you would cross a light-century in a single year of your own experience. (Though, of course, you could never regain the century that had passed at home, during which your friends grew old and died.) This would inevitably involve a hundredfold increase of mass. A Bussard engine, drawing on the hydrogen of space, could supply that. Indeed, it would be foolish to stop the engine and coast when you could go right on decreasing your tau.

Therefore, to reach other suns in a reasonable portion of your life expectancy: Accelerate continuously, right up to the interstellar midpoint, at which point you activate the decelerator system in the Bussard module and start slowing down again. You are limited by the speed of light, which you can never quite reach. But you are not limited in how close you can approach that speed. And thus you have no limit on your inverse tau factor.

Throughout her year at one gravity, the differences between *Leonora Christine* and the slow-moving stars had accumulated imperceptibly. Now the curve entered upon the steep part of its climb. Now, more and more, her folk measured the distance to their goal as shrinking, not simply because they traveled, but because, for them, the geometry of space was changing. More and more, they perceived natural processes in the outside universe as speeding up.

It was not yet spectacular. Indeed, the minimum tau in her flight plan, at midpoint, was to be somewhat above 0.015. But an instant came when a minute aboard her corresponded to sixty-one seconds in the rest of the galaxy. A while later, it corresponded to sixty-two. Then sixty-three . . . sixty-four . . . the ship time between such counts grew gradually but steadily less . . . sixty-five . . . sixty-six . . . sixty-seven . . . .

The first Christmas – Chanukah, New Year's, solstice festival season – that the crew spent together had come early in their voyage and was a feverish carnival. The second was quieter. People were settling down to their work and their fellows. Nevertheless, improvised ornaments glittered on all decks. The hobby rooms resounded, the scissors and needles clicked, the galley grew fragrant with spice, as everybody tried to make small gifts for everybody else. The hydroponics division found it could spare enough green vines and branches for an imitation tree in the gymnasium. From the enormous microtape library came films of snow and sleighs, recordings of carols. The thespian contingent rehearsed a pageant. Chef Carducci planned banquets. Commons and cabins rollicked with parties. By tacit agreement, no one mentioned that each second which passed laid Earth three hundred thousand kilometers farther behind.

Reymont made his way through a bustling recreation level. Some groups were stringing up the most newly made decorations. Nothing could be wasted, but aluminium-foil chains, blown-glass globes, wreaths twisted from bolts of cloth, were reclaimable. Others played games, chattered, offered drinks around, flirted, got boisterous. Through the chatter and laughter and shuffling, hum and crackle and rustle, music floated out of a loudspeaker:

'*Adeste, fideles,*
Laeti, triumphantes,
Venite, venite, in Bethlehem.'

Iwamoto Tetsuo, Hussein Sadek, Yeshu ben-Zvi, Mohandas Chidambaran, Phra Takh, or Kato M'Botu seemed to belong with it as much as Olga Sobieski or Johann Freiwald.

The machinist bellowed at Raymont: '*Guten Tag, mein lieber Schutzmann!* Come share my bottle!' He waved it in the air. His free arm was around Margarita Jimenes. Suspended above them was a slip of paper on which had been printed MISTLETOE.

Reymont halted. He got along well with Freiwald. 'Thank you, no,' he said. 'Have you seen Boris Fedoroff? I expected him to come here when he got off work.'

'N-no. I would expect it too, as lively as things are tonight. He's become a lot happier lately for some reason, hasn't he? What do you want of him?'

'Business matter.'

'Business, forever business,' Freiwald said. 'I swear your personal amusement is fretting. Me, I've got a better one.' He hugged Jimenes to him. She snuggled. 'Have you called his cabin?'

'Naturally. No response. Still, maybe – ' Reymont turned. 'I'll try there. Later I'll come back for that schnapps,' he added, already leaving.

He took the stairs down past crew level to the officers' deck. The music followed. ' – *Iesu, tibi sit gloria.*' The passageway was deserted. He pushed Fedoroff's chime button.

The engineer opened the door. He was clad in lounging pajamas. Behind him, a bottle of French wine, two glasses, and some Danish-style sandwiches waited on the dresser top. Surprise jarred him. He took a backward step. '*Chto –* you?'

'Could I speak with you?'

'Um-m-m.' Fedoroff's glance flickered. 'I expect a guest.'

Reymont grinned. 'That's obvious. Don't worry, I won't linger. But this is rather urgent.'

Fedoroff bridled. 'It cannot wait until I am on duty?'

'The thing is, it had better be discussed confidentially,' Reymont said. 'Captain Telander agrees.' He slipped around Fedoroff, into the cabin. 'An item was overlooked in the plans,' he went on, speaking fast. 'Our schedule has us changing over to high-acceleration mode on the seventh of January. You know better than I how that takes two or three days of preliminary work by your gang and considerable upsetting of everybody else's routine. Well, somehow the flight planners forgot that the sixth is important in West European tradition. Twelfth Night, the Eve of the Three Holy Kings, call it what you will, it climaxes the merrymaking part of the holidays. Last year celebrations were so riotous that nobody thought about it. But I learn that this year a final feast and dance, with the old rituals, is being talked of, as something that would be pleasant if only it were possible. Think what such a reminder of our origins can do to help morale. The skipper and I wish you'd check the feasibility of postponing high acceleration a few days.'

'Yes, yes, I will look into it.' Fedoroff urged Reymont toward the open door. 'Tomorrow, please – '

He was too late. Ingrid Lindgren came around its edge. She was in uniform, having hurried up from the bridge when her watch ended.

'*Gud!*' broke from her. She stopped dead.

'Why, why, Lindgren,' Fedoroff said frantically, 'what brings you here?'

Reymont had sucked in a single breath. Every expression went out of his face. He stood moveless, except that his fists clenched till nails dug into palms and skin stretched white across knuckles.

A new carol began.

Lindgren looked back and forth, between the men. Her own features were drained of blood. Abruptly, though, she straightened and said: 'No, Boris. We'll not lie.'

'It wouldn't help any more,' Reymont agreed without tone.

Fedoroff whirled on him. 'All right!' he cried. 'All right!

58

We have been together a few times. She's not your wife.'

'I never claimed she was,' Reymont answered, his eyes on her. 'I did intend to ask her to be, when we arrived.'

'Carl,' she whispered. 'I love you.'

'No doubt one partner gets boring,' Reymont said like winter. 'You felt the need of refreshment. Your privilege, of course. I did think you were above slinking behind my back.'

'Let her alone!' Fedoroff grabbed blindly for him.

The constable flowed aside. His hand chopped edge-on. The engineer gasped in anguish, collapsed to a seat on the bed, and caught his injured wrist in the other hand.

'It's not broken,' Seymont told him. 'However, if you don't stay where you are till I leave, I'll disable you.' He paused. Judiciously: 'That's not a challenge to your manhood. I know single combat the way you know nucleonics. Let's stay civilized. She's yours anyway, I suppose.'

'Carl.' Lindgren took a step and another toward him, reaching. Tears whipped down her cheeks.

He sketched a bow. 'I will remove my things from your cabin as soon as I have found a vacant berth.'

'No, Carl, Carl.' She clutched his tunic. 'I never imagined – Listen, Boris needed me. Yes, I admit it, I enjoyed being with him, but it was never deeper than friendship . . . help . . . while you – '

'Why didn't you tell me what you were doing? Wasn't I entitled to know?'

'You were, you were, but I was afraid – a few remarks you'd let drop – you *are* jealous – and it's so unnecessary, because you're the only one who counts.'

'I've been poor my whole life,' he said, 'and I do have a poor man's primitive morality, as well as some regard for privacy. On Earth there might be ways to make matters – not right again, really, but tolerable. I could fight my rival, or go away on a long trip, or you and I could both move elsewhere. None of that is possible here.'

'Can't you understand?' she implored.

'Can't you?' He had closed his fists anew. 'No,' he said, 'you honestly – I'll assume honestly – don't believe you did

59

me any harm. The years will be hard enough to get through without keeping up that kind of relationship.'

He disengaged her from him. 'Stop blubbering!' he barked.

She shuddered and grew rigid. Fedoroff growled. He started to rise. She waved him back.

'That's better.' Reymont went to the door. There he stood and faced them. 'We'll have no scenes, no intrigues, no grudges,' he stated. 'When fifty people are locked into one hull, everybody conducts himself right or everybody dies. Mister Engineer Fedoroff, Captain Telander and I would like your report on the subject I came to discuss as soon as can be managed. You might get the opinion of Miss First Officer Lindgren, bearing in mind that secrecy is desirable till we're ready to make an announcement one way or another.' For an instant, the pain and fury struck out of him. 'Our duty is to the ship, hell damn you!' Control clamped down. He clicked his heels. 'My apologies. Good evening.'

He left.

Fedoroff got up behind Lindgren and laid his arms around her. 'I am very sorry,' he said in his awkwardness. 'If I had guessed this might happen, I would never – '

'Not your fault, Boris.' She didn't move.

'If you would share quarters with me, I would be glad.'

'No, thank you,' she answered dully. 'I'm out of that game for the time being.' She released herself. 'I'd better go. Good night.' He stood alone with his sandwiches and wine.

> '*O holy child of Bethlehem,*
> *Descend to us, we pray.*'

The proper adjustments being made, *Leonora Christine* raised her acceleration a few days after Epiphany.

It would make no particular difference to the cosmic duration of her passage. In either case, she ran at the heels of light. But by decreasing tau faster, and reaching lower values of it at mid-point, the higher thrust appreciably shortened the shipboard time.

Extending her scoopfields more widely, intensifying the

thermonuclear fireball that trailed her trailing Bussard engine, the ship shifted over to three gravities. This would have added almost thirty meters per second per second to a low velocity. To her present speed, it added tiny increments which grew constantly tinier. That was in outside measurement. Inboard, she drove ahead at three gee; and that measurement was equally real.

Her human payload could not have taken it and lived long. The stress on heart, lungs, and specially on body fluid balance would have been too great. Drugs might have helped. Fortunately, there was a better way.

The forces that pushed her nearer and nearer to ultimate c were not merely enormous. Of necessity, they were precise. They were, indeed, so precise that their interaction with the outside universe – matter and its own force fields – could be held to a nearly constant resultant in spite of changes in those exterior conditions. Likewise, the driving energies could safely be coupled to similar, much weaker fields when the latter were established within the hull.

This linkage could then operate on the asymmetries of atoms and molecules to produce an acceleration uniform with that of the inside generator itself. In practice, though, the effect was left incomplete. One gravity was uncompensated.

Hence weight inboard remained at a steady Earth-surface value, no matter how high the rate at which the ship gained speed.

Such cushioning was only achievable at relativistic velocities. At an ordinary pace, their tau large, atoms were insufficiently massive, too skittish to get a good grip on. As they approached c, they grew heavier – not to themselves, but to everything outside their vessel – until the interplay of fields between cargo and cosmos could establish a stable configuration.

Three gravities was not the limit. With scoopfields fully extended, and in regions where matter occurred more densely than hereabouts, such as a nebula, she could have gone considerably higher. In this particular crossing, given the tenuousness of the local hydrogen, any possible gain in time was not enough – since the formula involves a hyperbolic function – to be worth reducing her safety margin. Other considerations, e.g., the optimization of mass intake versus the minimization of path length, had also entered into computing her flight pattern.

Thus, tau was no static multiplying factor. It was dynamic. Its work on mass, space, and time could be observed as a fundamental thing, creating a forever new relationship between men and the universe through which they fared.

In a shipboard hour that the calendar said was in April and the clock said was in morning, Reymont awoke. He didn't stir, blink, yawn, and stretch like most men. He sat up, immediately alert.

Chi-Yuen Ai-Ling had ended sleep earlier. His suddenness caught her kneeling in Asian fashion at the foot of the bed, regarding him with a seriousness altogether unlike her playful mood of the night before.

'Is anything wrong?' he demanded.

She had only shown startlement in a widening of eyes. After a moment, her smile came to slow life. 'I knew a tame hawk once,' she remarked. 'That is, it wasn't tame in dog fashion, but it hunted with its man and deigned to sit on his wrist. You come awake the same way.'

'Mph,' he said. 'I meant that worried look of yours.'

'Not worried, Charles. Thoughtful.'

He admired the sight of her. Unclad, she could never be called boyish. The curves of breast and flank were subtler than ordinary, but they were integral with the rest of her – not stuccoed on, as with too many women – and when she moved, they flowed. So did the light along her skin, which had the hue of the hills around San Francisco Bay in their summer, and the light in her hair, which had the smell of every summer day that ever was on Earth.

They were in his crew-level cabin half, screened off from his partner Foxe-Jameson. It made too drab a setting for her. Her own quarters were filled with beauty.

'What about?' he inquired.

'You. Us.'

'It was a gorgeous night.' He reached out to stroke her beneath the chin. She made purring noises. 'More?'

Her gravity returned. 'That's what I was wondering.' He cocked his brows. 'An understanding between us. We've had our flings. At least, you have had, in the past few months.' His face darkened. She went doggedly on: 'To myself, it wasn't that important; an occasional thing. I don't want to continue with it, really. If nothing else, those hints and attempts, the whole courtship rite, over and over . . . they interfere with my work. I'm developing some ideas about planetary cores. They need concentration. A lasting liaison would help.'

'I don't want to make any contracts,' he said grimly.

She caught his shoulders. 'I realize that. I'm not asking for one. Nor offering it. I have simply come to like you better each time we have talked, or danced, or spent a night. You are a quiet man, mostly; strong; courteous, to me at any rate. I could live happily with you – nothing exclusive on either side, only an alliance, for the whole ship to see – as long as we both want to.'

'Done!' he exclaimed, and kissed her.

'That quickly?' she asked, astonished.

'I'd given it some thought too. I'm also tired of chasing. You should be easy to live with.' He ran a hand down her side and thigh. 'Very easy.'

'How much of your heart is in that?' At once she laughed. 'No, I apologize, such questions are excluded . . . . Shall we move into my cabin? I know Maria Toomajian won't mind trading places with you. She keeps her part closed off anyway.'

'Fine,' he said. 'Sweetheart, we still have almost an hour before breakfast call – '

Leonora Christine was nearing the third year of her journey, or the tenth year as the stars counted time, when grief came upon her.

CHAPTER 7

An outside watcher, quiescent with respect to the stars, might have seen the thing before she did; for at her speed she must needs run half-blind. Even without better sensors than hers, he would have known of the disaster a few weeks ahead. But he would have had no way to cry his warning.

And there was no watcher anyhow: only night, bestrewn with multitudinous remote suns, the frosty cataract of the Milky Way and the rare phantom glimmer of a nebula or sister galaxy. Nine light-years from Sol, the ship was illimitably alone.

An automatic alarm roused Captain Telander. As he struggled upward from sleep, Lindgren's voice followed on the intercom: '*Kors i Herrens namn!*' The horror in it jerked him fully awake. Not stopping to acknowledge, he ran from his cabin. Nor would he have stopped to dress, had he been abed.

As it happened, he was clad. Lulled by the sameness of time, he had been reading a novel projected from the library and had dozed off in his chair. Then the jaws of the universe snapped shut.

He didn't notice the gaiety that now covered passageway bulkheads, or the springiness underfoot or the scent of roses and thundershowers. Loud in his awareness beat the engine vibrations. The stairs made a metal clatter beneath his haste, which the well flung back.

He emerged on the next level up and entered the bridge. Lindgren stood near the viewscope. It was not what counted; at this moment, it was almost a toy. What truth the ship could tell was in the instruments which glittered across the entire forward panel. But her eyes would not leave it.

The captain brushed past her. The warning which had caused him to be summoned was still blazoned on a screen linked to the astronomical computer. He read. The breath hissed between his teeth. His gaze went across the surrounding meters and displays. A slot clicked and extruded a printout. He snatched it. The letters and figures represented a quantification: decimal-point detail, after more data had come in and more calculation had been done. The basic Mene, Mene stood unchanged on the panel.

He stabbed the general alert button. Sirens wailed; echoes went ringing down the corridors. On the intercom he ordered all hands not on duty to report to commons with the passengers. After a moment, harshly, he added that channels would be open so that those people standing watch could also take part in the meeting.

'What are we going to do?' Lindgren cried into a sudden stillness.

'Very little, I fear.' Telander went to the viewscope. 'Is anything visible in this?'

'Barely. I think. Fourth quadrant.' She shut her eyes and turned from him.

He took for granted that she meant the projection for dead ahead, and peered into that. At high magnification, space leaped at him. The scene was somewhat blurred and distorted. Optical circuits were not able to compensate perfectly for speeds like this. But he saw starpoints, diamond, amethyst, ruby, topaz, emerald, a Fafnir's hoard. Near the center burned Beta Virginis. It should have looked very like the sun of home, but something of spectral shift got by to tinge it ice blue. And, yes, on the edge of perception . . . that wisp? That smoky cloudlet, to wipe out this ship and these fifty human lives?

Noise broke in on his concentration, shouts, footfalls, the sounds of fear. He straightened. 'I had better go aft,' he said, flat-voiced. 'I should consult Boris Fedoroff before addressing the others.' Lindgren moved to join him. 'No, keep the bridge.'

'Why?' Her temper stretched him. 'Regulations?'

He nodded. 'Yes. You have not been relieved.' A smile of sorts touched his lean face. 'Unless you believe in God, regulations are now the only comfort we have.'

*

65

In this moment, the drapes and murals of the gymnasium-auditorium had no more significance than the basketball goals or the bright casual clothes of the people. They had not taken time to unfold chairs. Everyone stood. Every gaze locked onto Telander while he mounted the stage. Nobody stirred save to breathe. Sweat glistened on countenances and could be smelled. The ship muttered around them.

Telander rested his fingers on the lectern. 'Ladies and gentlemen,' he said into their silence, 'I have bad news.' Quickly: 'Let me say at once that our prospects of survival are far from hopeless, judging by present information. We are in trouble, though. The risk was not unforeseen, but by its nature is one that cannot be provided against, at any rate not in our early stage of Bussard drive technology – '

'Get to the point, God damn it!' Norbert Williams shouted.

'Quiet, you,' said Reymont. Unlike most of them, who stood with male and female hands clutched together, he held apart, near the stage. To a drab coverall he had pinned his badge of authority.

'You can't – ' Someone must have nudged Williams, for he spluttered into silence.

Telander's frame grew visibly tenser. 'Instruments have . . . have detected an obstacle. A small nebula. Extremely small, a clot of dust and gas, no more than a few billion kilometers across. It is travelling at an abnormal velocity. Maybe it's a remnant of a larger thing cast out by a supernova, a remnant still held together by hydromagnetic forces. Or maybe it's a protostar. I do not know.

'The fact is, we are going to strike it. In about twenty-four hours, ship's time. What will happen then, I don't know either. With luck, we can ride out the impact and not suffer serious damage. Otherwise . . . if the fields become too overloaded to protect us . . . well, we knew this journey would have its hazards.'

He heard indrawn breaths, like his own on the bridge, and saw eyes grow white-rimmed, lips flutter, fingers trace signs in the air. He persisted: 'We cannot do much to prepare. A little battening down, yes; but in general, the ship is already as taut as can be. When the moment approaches, we will be in shock harness and space armor. So – The meeting is now open for discussion.' Williams' hand rocketed past the shoulder of tall M'Botu. 'Yes?'

The chemist's ruddiness showed indignation rather than fear. 'Mister Captain! The robot probe observed no dangers on this route. At least, it beamed back no hint of them. Right? Who's responsible for our blundering into this muck?'

Voices lifted toward a babble. 'Quiet!' Charles Reymont called. Though he didn't speak loud, he pushed the sound from his lungs in such a way that it struck. Several resentful glances were cast at him, but the talkers came to order.

'I thought I had explained,' Telander said. 'The cloud is minute by cosmic standards, nonluminous, undetectable at any large distance. It has a high velocity, scores of KPS. Thus, supposing the probe had taken our identical path, the nebulina would have been well offside at the time – more than fifty years ago, remember. Furthermore . . . we can be certain the probe did not go exactly as we are going. Besides the relative motion of Sol and Beta Virginis, consider the distance between. Thirty-two light-years is more than our poor minds can picture. The slightest variation in the curves taken from star to star means a difference of many astronomical units in the middle.'

'This thing couldn't have been predicted,' Reymont added. 'The chances were big against our running into it. Still, somebody has to draw the long odds now and then.'

Telander stiffened. 'I did not recognize you, Constable,' he said.

Reymont flushed. 'Captain, I was trying to expedite matters, so some snotbrains won't keep you here explaining the obvious till we smash.'

'No insults to shipmates, Constable. And kindly wait to be recognized before you speak.'

'I beg the captain's pardon.' Reymont folded his arms and blanked his features.

Telander said with care: 'Please do not be afraid to ask questions, however elementary they seem. You are all educated in the theory of interstellar astronautics. But I, whose profession this is, know how strange the paradoxes are, how hard to keep straight in one's mind. Best if everyone understands exactly what we are meeting . . . . Dr Glassgold?'

The molecular biologist lowered her hand and said timidly: 'Can't we – I mean – nebular objects like that, they would count as hard vacuums on Earth. Wouldn't they? And we, we are just under the speed of light, gaining more every second. And so more mass. Our inverse tau is about fifteen at the moment, I believe. That means our mass is enormous. So how can a bit of dust and gas stop us?'

'A good point,' Telander replied. 'If we are lucky, we will pass without too great hindrance. Not entirely. Remember, that dust and gas is moving equally fast with respect to us, with a corresponding increase of its mass.

'The force fields have to do work on it, directing the hydrogen into the ramjet system and diverting all matter from the hull. This action has its reaction on us. Moreover, it will take place extremely rapidly. What the fields can do in, say, an hour, they may not be able to do in a minute. We must hope that they can, and that the material components of the ship can endure the resultant stresses.

'I have spoken with Chief Engineer Fedoroff at his post. He thinks probably we will not suffer grave damage. He admits his opinion is a mere extrapolation. In a pioneering era, one learns chiefly by experience. Mr Iwamoto?'

'S-s-sst! I presume we have no possibility of avoidance? One day ship's time is about two weeks cosmic time, no? We have not a chance to go around this nebu – nebulina?'

'No, I fear not. In our own frame of reference, we are accelerating at approximately three gravities. In terms of the outside universe, however, that acceleration is not constant, but steadily decreasing. Therefore we cannot change course fast. Even a full vector normal to our velocity would not get us far enough aside before the encounter. Anyhow, we haven't the time to make the preparations for such a drastic alteration of flight pattern. Ah, Second Engineer M'Botu?'

'Might it help if we decelerated? We must keep one or another mode operative at all times, forward or backward thrust, to be sure. But I should think that deceleration now would soften the collision.'

'The computer has not made any recommendations about that. Probably the information is insufficient. At best, the percentage difference in speed would be slight. I fear ... I think we have no choice except to – ah – '

'Bull through,' Reymont said in English. Telander cast him a look of annoyance. Reymont didn't seem to mind.

As discussion progressed, though, his glance darted from speaker to speaker and the lines between mouth and nostrils deepened in his face. When at last Telander pronounced, 'Dismissed,' the constable did not return to Chi-Yuen. He pushed almost brutally through the uncertain milling of the rest and plucked the captain's sleeve.

'I think we had better hold a private talk, sir,' he declared. The choppiness he had been losing was back in his accent.

Telander said with a chill, 'Now is hardly the time to deny anyone access to facts, Constable.'

'Oh, call it politeness, that we go work by ourselves instead of bothering people,' Reymont answered impatiently.

Telander sighed. 'Come with me to the bridge, then. I'm too busy for special conferences.'

A couple of others seemed to feel differently, but Reymont drove them off with a glare and a bark. Telander must perforce smile a bit as he went out the door. 'You do have your uses,' he admitted.

'A parliamentary hatchet man?' Reymont said. 'I fear they'll be more call on me than that.'

'Conceivably on Beta Three. A specialist in rescue and disaster control might be welcome *when* we get there.'

'You're the one who's concealing facts, Captain. You're pretty badly shaken by what we're driving into. I suspect our chances are not quite as good as you pretended. Right?'

Telander looked around and did not reply until they were alone in the stairwell. He lowered his voice. 'I simply don't know. Nor does Fedoroff. No Bussard ship has been tested under conditions like those ahead of us. Obviously! We'll either get by in reasonable shape or we'll die. In the latter case, I don't imagine it'll be from radiation sickness. If any of that material penetrates the screens and hits us, it should wipe us out, a quick clean death. I saw no reason to make worse what hours remain for our people, by dwelling on that possibility.'

Reymont scowled. 'You overlook a third chance. We may survive, but in bad shape.'

'How the devil could we?'

'Hard to say. Perhaps we'll take such a buffeting that personnel are killed. Key personnel, whom we can ill afford to lose . . . not that fifty is any great number.' Reymont brooded. Footsteps thudded in the mumble of energies. 'They reacted well, on the whole,' he said. 'They were picked for courage and coolness, along with health and intelligence. In a few instances, the picking may not have been entirely successful. Suppose we do find ourselves, let's say, disabled. What next? How long will morale last, or sanity itself? I want to be ready to maintain discipline.'

'In that connection,' Telander responded, cold once more, 'please remember that you act under my orders and subject to the articles of the expedition.'

'Damnation!' Reymont exploded: 'What do you take me for? A would-be Mao? I'm requesting your authorization to deputize certain trustworthy men and prepare them quietly for emergencies. I'll issue them weapons, stunner type only. If nothing goes wrong – or if something does but everybody behaves himself – what have we lost?'

'Mutual trust,' the captain said.

They had come to the bridge. Reymont entered with his companion, arguing further. Telander made a hacking gesture to shut him up and strode toward the control console. 'Anything new?' he asked.

'Yes. The instruments have begun to draw a density map,' Lindgren answered. She had flinched on seeing Reymont and spoke mechanically, not looking at him. 'It is recommended – ' She pointed to the screens and the latest printout.

Telander studied them. 'Hm. We can pass through a slightly less thick region of the nebula, it seems, if we generate a lateral vector by activating the Number Three and Four decelerators in conjunction with the entire accelerator system. . . . A procedure with hazards of its own. This calls for discussion.' He flipped the intercom controls and spoke briefly to Fedoroff and Boudreau. 'In the plotting room. On the double!'

He turned to go. 'Captain – ' Reymont attempted.

'Not now,' Telander said. His legs scissored across the deck.

'But – '

'The answer is no.' Telander vanished out the door.

Reymont stood where he was, head lowered and shoulders hunched as if to charge. But he had nowhere to go. Ingrid Lindgren regarded him for a time that shivered – a minute or more, ship's chronology, which was a quarter hour in the lives of the stars and planets – before she said, very softly, 'What did you want of him?'

'Oh.' Reymont fell into a normal posture. 'His order to recruit a police reserve. He gave me something stupid about my not trusting my fellows.'

Their eyes clashed. 'And not letting them alone in what may be their final hours,' she said. It was the first occasion since their breach that they had stopped addressing each other with entire correctness.

'I know.' Reymont spat out his words. 'There's little for them to do, they think, except wait. So they'll spend the time . . . talking; reading favorite poems; eating favorite foods, with an extra wine ration, Earthside bottles; playing music, opera and ballet and theater tapes, or in some cases something livelier, maybe bawdier; making love. Especially making love.'

'Is that bad?' she asked. 'If we must go out, shouldn't we do so in a civilized, decent, life-loving way?'

'By being a trifle less civilized, et cetera, we might increase our chance of not going out.'

'Are you that afraid to die?'

'No. I simply like to live.'

'I wonder,' she said. 'I suppose you can't help your crudeness. You have that kind of background. What about your unwillingness to overcome it, though?'

'Frankly,' he answered, 'having seen what education and culture make people into, I'm less and less interested in acquiring them.'

The spirit gave way in her. Her eyes blurred, she reached out toward him and said, 'Oh, Carl, are we going to fight the same old fight over again, now in what's maybe our last day alive?' He stood rigid. She went on, fast: 'I loved you. I wanted you for my life's partner, the father of my children, whether on Beta Three or Earth. But we're so alone, all of us, here between the stars. We have to give what kindness we can, and take it, or we're worse than dead.'

'Unless we can control our emotions.'

'Do you think there was any emotion . . . anything but friendship, and wanting to help him get over his hurt, and – and a wish to make sure he did *not* fall seriously in love with me – with Boris? And the articles state, in as many words, we can't have formal marriages en route, because we're too constricted and deprived as is – '

'So you and I terminated a relationship which had become unsatisfactory.'

'You made plenty of others!' she flared.

'For a while. Till I found Ai-Ling. Whereas you've taken to sleeping around again.'

'I have normal needs. I've not settled down . . . committed myself' – she gulped – 'like you.'

'Nor I, except that one does not abandon a partner when the going gets bad.' Reymont shrugged. 'No matter. As you implied, we're both free individuals. It wasn't easy, but I've finally convinced myself it's not sensible or right to carry a grudge because you and Fedoroff exercised that freedom. Don't let me spoil your fun after you go off watch.'

'Nor I yours.' She brushed violently at her eyes.

'As a matter of fact, I'll be occupied till nearly the last

minute. Since I wasn't allowed to deputize, I'm going to ask for volunteers.'

'You can't!'

'I wasn't actually forbidden. I'll brace a few men, in private, who're likely to agree. We'll constitute ourselves a stand-by force, alerted to do whatever we can that's needed. Do you mean to tell the captain?'

She turned from him. 'No,' she said. 'Please go away.'

His boots clacked off down the corridor.

CHAPTER 8

Everything that could be done had been. Now, spacesuited, strapped into safety cocoons that were anchored to the beds, the folk of *Leonora Christine* waited for impact. Some left their helmet radios on so they could talk with their roommates; others preferred solitude. With head secured, no one could see another, nor anything except the bareness above his faceplate.

Reymont and Chi-Yuen's quarters felt more cheerless than most. She had stowed away the silk draperies that softened bulkheads and overhead, the low-legged table she had made to hold a Han Dynasty bowl with water and a single stone, the scroll with its serene mountainscape and her grandfather's calligraphy, the clothes, the sewing kit, the bamboo flute. Fluorolight fell bleak on unpainted surfaces.

They had been silent awhile, though their sets were tuned. He listened to her breath and the slow knocking of his own heart. 'Charles,' she said finally.

'Yes?' He spoke with the same quietness.

'It has been good with you. I wish I could touch you.'

'Likewise.'

'There is a way. Let me touch your self.' Taken aback, he

had no ready reply. She continued: 'You have always held most of you hidden. I don't imagine I'm the first woman to tell you so.'

'You aren't.' She could hear the difficulty he had in saying it.

'Are you certain you weren't making a mistake?'

'What's to explain? I've scant use for those types whose chief interest is their grubbly little personal neuroses. Not in a universe as rich as this.'

'You never mentioned your childhood, for instance,' she said. 'I shared mine with you.'

He snorted out a kind of mirth. 'Consider yourself spared. The Polyugorsk low-levels weren't nice.'

'I've heard about conditions there. I never quite understood how they came about.'

'The Control Authority couldn't act. No danger to world peace. The local bosses were too useful in too many ways to higher national figures to be thrown out. Like some of the war lords in your country, I imagine, or the Leopards on Mars before fighting got provoked. A lot of money to be had in the Antarctic, for those who didn't mind gutting the last resources, killing the last wildlife, raping the last white wilderness – ' He stopped. His voice had been rising. 'Well, that's all behind us. I wonder if the human race will do any better on Beta Three. I rather doubt it.'

'How did you learn to care about such things?' she asked mutedly.

'A teacher, to begin with. My father was killed when I was young, and by the time I was twelve, my mother had nearly finished going down the drain. We had this one man, however, Mr Melikot, an Abyssinian, I don't know how he ended up in our hellhole of a school, but he lived for us and for what he taught, we felt it and our brains came awake. . . . I'm not certain if he did me a favor. I got to thinking and reading, and that got me into talking and doing, and that got me into trouble till I had to skip for Mars, never mind how. . . . Yes, I suppose it was a favor in the long run.

'You see,' she said, smiling in her helmet, 'it isn't hard to take off a mask.'

74

'What do you mean?' he demanded. 'I'm trying to oblige you, no more.'

'Because we may soon be dead. That tells me something about you also, Charles. I begin to see the why of things, the man behind them. Why they say you were honest but tight-fisted with money in the Solar System, to name a trivial detail. Why you're often gruff, and never try to dress well though it would look good on you, and hide that possessiveness of yours behind a "Go your own way if you don't want to go mine" that can be really freezing, and – '

'Hold on! A psychoanalysis, from a few elementary facts about when I was a kid?'

'Oh no, no. That would be ridiculous, I agree. But a bit of understanding, from the way you told them. A wolf in search of a den.'

'Enough!'

'Of course. I'm happy that you – No further, not ever again, unless you want.' Chi-Yuen's figure of speech evidently lingered in her consciousness, for she mused: 'I miss animals. More than I expected. We had carp and songbirds in my parents' house. Jacques and I had a cat in Paris. I never realized till we traveled this far, how big a part of the world the rest of the animal creation is. Crickets in summer nights, a butterfly, a humming-bird, fish jumping in the water, sparrows in a street, horses with velvet noses and warm smell – Do you think we will find anything like Earth's animals on Beta Three?'

The ship struck.

It was too swiftly changing a pattern of assault too great. The delicate dance of energies which balanced out acceleration pressures could not be continued. Its computer choreographers directed a circuit to break, shutting off that particular system, before positive feedback wrecked it.

Those aboard felt weight shift and change. A troll sat on each chest and choked each throat. Darkness went ragged before eyes. Sweat burst forth, hearts slugged, pulses brawled. That noise was answered by the ship, a metal groan, a rip and a crash. She was not meant for stresses like these. Her safety factors were small; mass was too precious. And she rammed hydrogen atoms swollen to the heaviness of nitrogen or oxygen, dust particles bloated into meteoroids. Velocity had flattened the cloud longitudinally, it was thin, she tore through in minutes. But by that same token, the nebulina was no longer a cloud to her. It was a well-nigh solid wall.

Her outside force-screens absorbed the battering, flung matter aside in turbulent streams, protected the hull from everything except slowdown drag. Reaction was inevitable, on the fields themselves and hence on the devices which, borne outside, produced and controlled them. Frameworks crumpled. Electronic components fused. Cryogenic liquids boiled from shattered containers.

So one of the thermonuclear fires went out.

The stars saw the event differently. They saw a tenuous murky mass struck by an object incredibly swift and dense. Hydromagnetic forces snatched at atoms, whirled them about, ionized them, cast them together. Radiation flashed. The object was encompassed in a meteor blaze. During the hour of its passage, it bored a tunnel through the nebulina. That tunnel was wider than the drill, because a shock wave spread outward – and outward and outward, destroying what stability there had been, casting substance forth in gouts and tatters.

If a sun and planets had been in embryo here, they would now never form.

The invader passed. It had not lost much speed. Accelerating once more, it dwindled away toward remoter stars.

CHAPTER 9

Reymont struggled back to wakefulness. He could not have been darkened long. Could he? Sound had ceased. Was he deafened? Had the air puffed out of some hole into space? Were the screens down, had gamma-colored death already sleeted through him?

No. When he listened, he made out the familiar low beat of power. The fluoropanel shone steadily in his vision. The shadow of his cocoon fell on a bulkhead and had the blurred edges which betokened ample atmosphere. Weight had returned to a single gee. Most of the ship's automata, at least, must be functioning. 'To hell with melodrama,' he heard himself say. His voice came as if from far off, a stranger's. 'We've got work.'

He fumbled with his harness. Muscles throbbed and ached. A trickle of blood ran over his mouth, tasting salty. Or was that sweat? *Nichevo*. He was operational. He crawled free, opened his helmet, sniffed – slight smell of scorch and ozone, nothing serious – and gusted one deep sigh.

The cabin was a mare's nest. Dresser drawers had burst open and scattered their contents. He didn't notice particularly. Chi-Yuen hadn't answered his queries. He waded through strewn garments to the slight form. Slipping off his gauntlets, he unlatched her faceplate. Her breathing sounded normal, no wheeze or gurgle to suggest internal injuries. When he peeled back an eyelid, the pupil was broad. Probably she had just fainted. He shucked his armor, located his stun pistol, and strapped it on. Others might need help worse. He went out.

Boris Fedoroff clattered down the stairs. 'How goes it?' Reymont hailed.

'I am on my way to see,' the engineer tossed back, and disappeared.

Reymont grinned sourly and pushed into Johann

Freiwald's cabin half. The German had removed his space-suit too and sat slumped on his bed. '*Raus mit dir,*' Reymont said.

'I have a headache like carpenters in my skull,' Freiwald protested.

'You offered to be in our squad. I thought you were a man.'

Freiwald gave Reymont a resentful glance but was stung into motion.

The constable's recruits were busy for the next hour. The regular spacemen were busier yet, inspecting, measuring, conferring in hushed tones. That gave them little chance to feel pain or let terror grow. The scientists and technicians had no such anodyne. From the fact that they were alive and the ship apparently working as before, they might have drawn happiness . . . only why didn't Telander make an announcement? Reymont bullied them into commons, started some making coffee and others attending to the most heavily bruised. At last he felt free to head for the bridge.

He stopped to look in on Chi-Yuen, as he had done at intervals. She was finally aware, had unharnessed but collapsed on her mattress before getting all armor off. A tiny light kindled in her when she saw him. 'Charles,' she susurrated.

'How are you?' he asked.

'I hurt, and I don't seem to have any strength, but – '

He stripped away the rest of her spacesuit. She winced at his roughness. 'Without this load, you should be able to get up to the gym,' he said. 'Dr Latvala can check you. No one else was too badly hammered, so it's unlikely you were.' He kissed her, a brief meaningless brush of lips. 'Sorry to be this unchivalrous. I'm in a hurry.'

He went on. The bridge door was closed. He knocked. Fedoroff boomed from within, 'No admittance. Wait for the captain to address you.'

'This is the constable,' Reymont answered.

'Well, go carry out your duties.'

'I've assembled the passengers. They're getting over being stunned. They're beginning to realize something isn't right. Not knowing what, in their present condition, will crack them open. Maybe we won't be able to glue the pieces back together.'

'Tell them a report will be issued shortly,' Telander called without steadiness.

'Shouldn't you tell them, sir? The intercom's working, isn't it? Tell them you're making exact assessments of damage in order to lay out a program for prompt repair. But I suggest, Mr Captain, you first let me in to help you find words for explaining the disaster.'

The door flew wide. Fedoroff grabbed Reymont's arm and tried to pull him through. Reymont yanked free, a judo release. His hand lifted, ready to chop. 'Don't ever do that,' he said. He stepped into the bridge and closed the door himself.

Fedoroff growled and doubled his fists. Lindgren hurried to him. 'No, Boris,' she begged. 'Please.' The Russian subsided, stiffly. They glared at Reymont in the thrumming stillness: captain, first officer, chief engineer, navigation officer, biosystems director. He glanced past them. The panels had suffered, various meter needles twisted, screens broken, wiring torn loose.

'Is that the trouble?' he asked, pointing.

'No,' said Boudreau, the navigator. 'We have replacements.'

Reymont sought the viewscope. The compensator circuits were equally dead. He moved on to the electronic periscope and put his face inside its hood.

A hemispheric simulacrum sprang from the darkness at him, the distorted scene he would have witnessed outside on the hull. The stars were crowded forward, streaming thinly amidships; they shone steel blue, violet, X ray. Aft the patterns approached what had once been familiar – but not very closely, and those suns were reddened, like embers, as if time were snuffing them out. Reymont shuddered a little and drew his head back into the cozy smallness of the bridge.

'Well?' he said.

'The decelerator system – ' Telander braced himself. 'We can't stop.'

Reymont went expressionless. 'Go on.'

Fedoroff spoke. His words fell contemptuous. 'You will recall, I trust, we had activated the decelerator part of the Bussard module to produce and operate two units. Their system is distinct from the accelerators, since to slow down we do not push gas through a ramjet but reverse its momentum.'

Reymont did not stir at the insult. Lindgren caught her breath. After a moment Fedoroff sagged.

'Well,' he said tiredly, 'the accelerators were also in use, at a much higher level of power. Doubtless on that account, their field strength protected them. The decelerators – Out. Wrecked.'

'How?'

'We can only determine that there has been material damage to their exterior controls and generators, and that the thermonuclear reaction which energized them is extinguished. Since the meters to the system aren't reporting – must be smashed -- we can't tell exactly what is wrong.'

Fedoroff looked at the deck. His words ran on, more soliloquy than report. A desperate man will rehearse obvious facts over and over. 'In the nature of the case, the decelerators must have been subjected to greater stress than the accelerators. I would guess that those forces, reacting through the hydromagnetic fields, broke the material assembly in that part of the Bussard module.

'No doubt we could make repairs if we could go outside. But we'd have to come too near the fireball of the accelerator power core in its own magnetic bottle. The radiation would kill us before we could do any useful work. The same is true for any remote-control robot we might build. You know what radiation at that level does to transistors, for instance. Not to mention inductive effects of the force fields.

'And, of course, we can't shut off the accelerators. That would mean shutting off the whole set of fields, including the screens, which only an outside power core can maintain. At our speed, hydrogen bombardment would release enough gamma rays and ions to fry everybody aboard within a minute.'

He fell silent, less like a man ending a lecture than a machine running down.

'Have we no directional control whatsoever?' Reymont asked, still toneless.

'Yes, yes, we do have that,' Boudreau said. 'The accelerator pattern can be varied. We can damp down any of the four venturis and boost up any others – get a sidewise as well as a forward vector. But don't you see, no matter what path we take, we must continue accelerating or we die.'

'Accelerating forever,' Telander said.

'At least,' Lindgren whispered, 'we can stay in the galaxy. Swing around and around its heart.' Her gaze went to the periscope, and they knew what she thought of: behind that curtain of strange blue stars, blackness, intergalactic void, an ultimate exile. 'At least . . . we can grow old . . . with suns around us. Even if we can't ever touch a planet again.'

Telander's features writhed. 'How do I tell our people?' he croaked.

'We have no hope,' Reymont said. It was hardly a question.

'None,' Fedoroff replied.

'Oh, we can live out our lives – reach a reasonable age, if not quite what antisenescence would normally permit,' said Pereira. 'The biosystems and organocycle apparatus are intact. We could actually increase their productivity. Do not fear immediate hunger or thirst or suffocation. True, the closed ecology, the reclamations, are not 100 per cent efficient. They will suffer slow losses, slow degrading. A spaceship is not a world. Man is not quite the clever designer and large-scale builder that God is.' His smile was ghastly. 'I do not advise that we have children. They would be trying to breathe things like acetone, while getting along without things like phosphorus and smothering in things like earwax and belly-button lint. But I imagine we can get fifty years out of our gadgets. Under the circumstances, that seems ample to me.'

Lindgren said from nightmare, staring at a bulkhead as if she could see through: 'When the last of us dies – We must put in an automatic cutoff. The ship must not keep on after our deaths. Let the radiation do what it will, let cosmic friction break her to bits and let the bits drift off yonder.'

'Why?' asked Reymont.

'Isn't it obvious? If we throw ourselves into a circular path ... consuming hydrogen, always traveling faster, running tau down and down as the thousands of years pass ... we get more massive. We could end by devouring the galaxy.'

'No, not that,' said Telander. He retreated into pedantry. 'I have seen calculations. Somebody did worry once about a Bussard craft getting out of control. But as Mr Pereira remarked, any human work is insignificant out here. Tau would have to become something like, shall we say, ten to the minus twentieth power before the ship's mass was equal to that of a minor star. And the odds are always literally astronomical against her colliding with anything more important than a nebula. Besides, we know the universe is finite in time as well as space. It would stop expanding and collapse before our tau got that low. We are going to die. But the cosmos is safe from us.'

'How long can we live?' Lindgren wondered. She cut Pereira off. 'I don't mean potentially. If you say half a century, I believe you. But I think in a year or two we will stop eating, or cut our throats, or agree to turn the accelerators off.'

'Not if I can help it,' Reymont snapped.

She gave him a dreary look. 'Do you mean you would continue – not just barred from man, from living Earth, but from the whole of creation?'

He regarded her steadily in return. His right hand rested on his gun butt. 'Don't you have that much guts?' he replied.

'Fifty years inside this flying coffin!' she almost screamed. 'How many will that be outside?'

'Easy,' Fedoroff warned, and took her around the waist. She clung to him and snatched after air.

Boudreau said, as carefully dry as Telander: 'The time

relationship appears to be somewhat academic to us, *n'est-ce pas*? It depends on what course we take. If we let ourselves continue straight outwards, naturally we will encounter a thinner medium. The rate of decrease of tau will grow proportionately smaller as we enter intergalactic space. Contrariwise, if we try for a cyclical path taking us through the densest hydrogen concentrations, we could get a very large inverse tau. We might see billions of years go by. That could be quite wonderful.' His smile was forced, a flash in the spade beard. 'We have each other too. A goodly company. I am with Charles. There are better ways to live but also worse ones.'

Lindgren hid against Fedoroff's breast. He held her, patted her with a clumsy hand. After a while (an hour or so in the history of the stars) she raised her face again.

'I'm sorry,' she gulped. 'You're right. We do have each other.' Her glance went among them, ending at Reymont.

'How shall I tell them?' the captain beseeched.

'I suggest you do not,' Reymont answered. 'Have the first officer break the news.'

'What?' Lindgren said.

'You are *simpático*,' he answered. 'I remember.'

She moved from Fedoroff's loosened grasp, a step toward Reymont.

Abruptly the constable tautened. He stood for a second as if blind, before he whirled from her and confronted the navigator.

'Hoy!' he exclaimed. 'I've gotten an idea. Do you know – '

'If you think I should – ' Lindgren had begun to say.

'Not now,' Reymont told her. 'Auguste, come over to the desk. We have a bit of figuring to do . . . fast!'

CHAPTER 10

The silence went on and on. Ingrid Lindgren stared from the stage, where she stood with Lars Telander, down at her people. They looked back at her. And not a one in that chamber could find words.

Hers had been well chosen. The truth was less savage in her throat than in any man's. But when she came to her planned midpoint – 'We have lost Earth, lost Beta Three, lost the mankind we belonged to. We have left to us courage, love, and, yes, hope' – she could not continue. She stood with lip caught between teeth, fingers twisted together, and the slow tears flowed from her eyes.

Telander stirred. 'Ah . . . if you will,' he tried. 'Kindly pay attention. A means does exist . . .' The ship jeered at him in her tone of distant lightnings.

Glassgold broke. She did not weep loudly, but her struggle to stop made the sound more dreadful. M'Botu, beside her, attempted consolation. He, though, had clamped such stoicism on himself that he might as well have been a robot. Iwamoto withdrew several paces from them both, from them all; one could see how he pulled his soul into some nirvana with a lock on its door. Williams shook his fist at the overhead and cursed. Another voice, female, started to keen. A woman considered the man with whom she had been keeping company, said, 'You, for my whole life?' and stalked from him. He tried to follow her and bumped into a crewman who snarled and offered to fight if he didn't apologize. A seething went through the entire human mass.

'Listen to me,' Telander said. 'Please listen.'

Reymont shook loose the arm which Chi-Yuen Ai-Ling held, where they stood in the first row, and jumped onto the stage. 'You'll never bring them around that way,' he declared *sotto voce*. 'You're used to disciplined professionals.

Let me handle these civilians.' He turned on them. 'Quiet, there!' Echoes bounced around his roar. 'Shut your hatches. Act like adults for once. We haven't the personnel to change your diapers for you.'

Williams yelped with resentment. M'Botu bared teeth. Reymont drew his stunner. 'Hold your places!' He dropped his vocal volume, but everyone heard him. 'The first of you to move gets knocked out. Afterward we'll court-martial him. I'm the constable of this expedition, and I intend to maintain order and effective co-operation.' He leered. 'If you feel I exceed my authority, you're welcome to file a complaint with the appropriate bureau in Stockholm. For now, you'll listen!'

His tongue-lashing activated their adrenals. With heightened vigor came self-possession. They glowered but waited alertly.

'Good.' Reymont turned mild and holstered his weapon. 'We'll say no more about this. I realize you've had a shock which none of you were prepared psychologically to meet. Nevertheless, we've got a problem. And it has a solution, if we can work together. I repeat: if.'

Lindgren had swallowed her weeping. 'I think I was supposed to – ' she said. He shook his head at her and went on:

'We can't repair the decelerators because we can't turn off the accelerators. The reason is, as you've been told, at high speeds we must have the force fields of one system or the other to shield us from interstellar gas. So it looks as if we're bottled in this hull. Well, I don't like the prospect either, though I believe we could endure it. Medieval monks accepted worse.

'Discussing it in the bridge, however, we got a thought. A possibility of escape, if we have the nerve and determination. Navigation Officer Boudreau ran a preliminary check for me. Afterward we called in Professor Nilsson for an expert opinion.'

The astronomer harrumphed and looked important. Jane Sadler seemed less impressed than others.

'We have a chance of success,' Reymont informed them.

A sound like a wind passed through the assembly. 'Don't make us wait!' cried a young man's voice.

'I'm glad to see some spirit,' Reymont said. 'It'll have to be kept on a tight rein, though, or we're finished. To make this as short as I can – afterward Captain Telander and the specialists will go into detail – here's the idea.'

His delivery might have been used to describe a new method of bookkeeping. 'If we can find a region where gas is practically nonexistent, we can safely shut down the fields, and our engineers can go outside and repair the decelerator system. Astronomical data are not as precise as we'd like. However, apparently throughout the galaxy and even in nearby intergalactic space, the medium is too dense. Much thinner out there than here, of course; still, so thick, in terms of atoms struck per second, as to kill us without our protection.

'Now galaxies generally occur in clusters. Our galaxy, the Magellanic Clouds, M31 in Andromeda, and thirteen others, large and small, make up one such group. The volume it occupies is about six million light-years across. Beyond them is an enormously greater distance to the next galactic family. By coincidence, it's in Virgo too: forty million light-years from here.

'In that stretch, we hope, the gas is thin enough for us not to need shielding.'

Babble tried to break out afresh. Reymont lifted both hands. He actually laughed. 'Wait, wait!' he called. 'Don't bother. I know what you want to say. Forty million light-years is impossible. We haven't the tau for it. A ratio of fifty, or a hundred, or a thousand, does us no good. Agreed. *But.*'

The last word stopped them. He filled his lungs. 'But remember,' he said, 'we have no limit on our inverse tau. We can accelerate at a lot more than three gee, too, if we widen our scoopfields and choose a path through sections of this galaxy where matter is dense. The exact parameters we've been using were determined by our course to Beta Virginis. The ship isn't restricted to them. Navigator Boudreau and Professor Nilsson estimate we can travel at an average of ten gee, quite likely more. Engineer Fedoroff is reasonably sure the accelerator system can stand that, after certain modifications he knows he can make.

'So. The gentlemen made rough calculations. Their results indicate we can swing halfway around the galaxy, spiraling inward till we plunge straight through its middle and out again on this side. We'd be slow about any course change anyway. We can't turn on a ten-*öre* coin at our speed! And this'll enable us to acquire the necessary tau. Don't forget, that'll decrease constantly. Our transit to Beta Vee would have been a lot quicker if we hadn't meant to stop there: if, instead of braking at mid-passage, we'd simply kept cramming on velocity.

'Navigator Boudreau estimates – estimates, mind you; we'll have to gather data as we go; but a good, informed guess – considering the speed we already have, he thinks we can finish with this galaxy and head out beyond it in a year or two.'

'How long cosmic time?' sounded from the gathering.

'Who cares?' Reymont retorted. 'You know the dimensions. The galactic disk is about a hundred thousand light-years across. At present we're thirty thousand from the center. One or two hundred millennia altogether? Who can tell? It'll depend on what path we take, which in turn will depend on what long-range observation can show us.'

He stabbed a finger at them. 'I know. You wonder, what if we hit a cloud such as got us into this miserable situation? I have two answers for that. First, we have to take some risks. But second, as our tau gets less and less, we'll be able to *use* regions which are denser and denser. We'll have too much mass to be affected as we were this time. Do you see? The more we have, the more we can get, and the faster we can get it in ship's time. We may conceivably leave the galaxy with an inverse tau on the order of a hundred million. In that case, by our clocks we'll be outside this entire galactic family in days!'

'How do we get back?' Glassgold said – but vigilant and interested.

'We don't,' Reymont admitted. 'We keep on to the Virgo cluster. There we reverse the process, decelerate, enter one of the member galaxies, bring our tau up to something sensible, and start looking for a planet where we can live.

'Yes, yes, yes!' he rapped into the renewed surf of their speech. 'Millions of years in the future. Millions of light-years hence. The human race most likely extinct . . . in this corner of the universe. Well, can't we start over, in another place and time? Or would you rather sit in a metal shell feeling sorry for yourselves, till you grow senile and die childless? Unless you can't stand the gaff and blow out your brains. I'm for going on as long as strength lasts. I think enough of this group to believe you will agree. Will anyone who feels differently be so good as to get out of our way?'

He stalked from the stage. 'Ah . . . Navigation Officer Boudreau, Chief Engineer Fedoroff, Professor Nilsson,' Telander said. 'Will you come here? Ladies and gentlemen, the meeting is open for general discussions – '

Chi-Yuen hugged Reymont. 'You were marvelous,' she sobbed.

His mouth tightened. He looked from her, from Lindgren, across the assemblage, to the enclosing bulkheads. 'Thanks,' he replied curtly. 'Wasn't much.'

'Oh, but it was. You gave us back hope. I am honored to live with you.'

He didn't seem to hear. 'Anybody could have presented a shiny new idea,' he said. 'They'll grasp at anything, right now. I only expedited matters. When they accept the program, that's when the real trouble begins.'

CHAPTER 11

Force fields shifted about. They were not static tubes and walls. What formed them was the incessant interplay of electromagnetic pulses, whose production, propagation, and heterodyning must be under control at every nanosecond, from the quantum level to the cosmic. As exterior conditions – matter density, radiation, impinging field strengths, gravitational space-curvature – changed, instant by instant, their reaction on the ship's immaterial web was registered; data were fed into the computers; handling a thousand simultaneous Fourier series as the smallest of their tasks, these machines sent back their answers; the generating and controlling devices, swimming aft of the hull in a vortex of their own output, made their supple adjustments. Into this homeostasis, this tightrope walk across the chance of a response that was improper or merely tardy – which would mean distortion and collapse of the fields, novalike destruction of the ship – entered a human command. It became part of the data. A starboard intake widened, a port intake throttled back: carefully, carefully. *Leonora Christine* swung around onto her new course.

The stars saw the ponderous movement of a steadily larger and more flattened mass, taking months and years before the deviation from its original track was significant. Not that the object whereon they shone was slow. It was a planet-sized shell of incandescence, where atoms were seized by its outermost force-fringes and excited into thermal, fluorescent, synchrotron radiation. And it came barely behind the wave front which announced its march. But the ship's luminosity was soon lost across light-years. Her passage crawled through abysses which seemingly had no end.

In her own time, the story was another. She moved in a universe increasingly foreign – more rapidly aging, more massive, more compressed. Thus the rate at which she could gulp down hydrogen, burn part of it to energy and hurl the rest off in a million-kilometer jet flame . . . that rate kept waxing for her. Each minute, as counted by her clocks, took a larger fraction off her tau than the last minute had done.

Inboard, nothing changed. Air and metal still carried the pulse of acceleration, whose net internal drag still stood at an even one gravity. The interior power plant continued to give light, electricity, equable temperatures. The biosystems and organocycles reclaimed oxygen and water, processed waste, manufactured food, supported life. Entropy increased. People grew older at the ancient rate of sixty seconds per minute, sixty minutes per hour.

Yet those hours were always less related to the hours and years which passed outside. Loneliness closed on the ship like fingers.

Jane Sadler executed a balestra. Johann Freiwald sought to parry. Her foil rang against his in a beat. Immediately, she thrust. '*Touché!*' he acknowledged. Laughing behind his mask: 'That would have skewered my left lung in a real duel. You have passed your examination.'

'None too soon,' she panted. 'I'd . . . have . . . been out of air . . . 'nother minute. Knees like rubber.'

'No more this evening,' Freiwald decided.

They took off their head protection. Sweat gleamed on her face and plastered hair to brow; her breath was noisy; but her eyes sparkled. 'Some workout!' She flopped onto a chair. Freiwald joined her. This late in the ship's evening, they had the gymnasium to themselves. It felt huge and hollow, making them sit close together.

'You will find it easier with other women,' Freiwald told her. 'I think you had better start them soon.'

'Me? Instruct a female fencing class at my stage?'

'I will continue to work out with you,' Freiwald said. 'You can stay ahead of your pupils. Don't you see, I must begin with the men. And if the sport draws as much interest as I would like, it will take time to make the equipment. Besides more masks and foils, we need épées and sabers. We cannot delay.'

Sadler's merriment faded. She gave him a studying look. 'You didn't propose this of your own accord? I'd assumed, you being the only person who'd fenced back on Earth, you wanted partners.'

'It was Constable Reymont's idea, when I happened to mention my wish. He arranged that stock be issued me to produce the gear. You see, we must maintain physical fitness – '

'And distract ourselves from the bind we're in,' she said harshly.

'A sound physique helps keep a sound mind. If you go to bed tired, you don't lie awake brooding.'

'Yes, I know. Elof – ' Sadler stopped.

'Professor Nilsson is perhaps too engaged in his work,' Freiwald dared say. His gaze left her, and he flexed the blade between his hands.

'He'd better be! Unless he can develop improved astronomical instrumentation, we can't plot an extragalactic trajectory on anything except guesswork.'

'True. True. I would suggest, Jane, your man might benefit, even in his profession, if he would take exercise.'

It was forced from her: 'He's getting harder to live with every day.' She took the offensive. 'So Reymont's appointed you coach.'

'Informally,' Freiwald said. 'He urged me to take leadership, develop new, attractive sports – Well, I *am* one of his unofficial deputies.'

'Uh-huh. And he himself can't. They'd see his motives, they'd think of him as a drillmaster, the fun would be gone, and they'd stay away by dozens.' Sadler smiled. 'Okay, Johann. Count me in on your conspiracy.'

She offered her hand. He took it. The clasp continued.

'Let's get out of this wet padding and into a wet swimming pool,' she proposed.

He replied scratchily: 'No, thank you. Not tonight. We would be alone. I don't dare that any longer, Jane.'

*

Leonora Christine encountered another region of increased matter density. It was more tenuous than the nebulina which had caused her trouble, and she ran it without difficulty. But it reached for many parsecs. Her tau shrank at a pace which in her own chronology was stupefying. By the time she emerged, she was going so fast that the normal one atom per cubic centimeter counted for about as much as the cloud had done. Not only did she keep the speed she had gained, she kept the acceleration.

Her folk continued regardless to follow Earth's calendar, including observances for the tiny congregations of different religions. Each seventh morning, Captain Telander led his handful of Protestants in divine service.

On a particular Sunday, he had asked Ingrid Lindgren to meet him in his cabin afterward. She was waiting there when he entered. Her fairness and a short red gown cast her vivid against books, desk, papers. Though he rated a double section to himself, its austerity was relieved by little except a few pictures of family and a half-built model of a clipper ship.

'Good morning,' he said with accustomed solemnity. He laid down his Bible and loosened the collar of his dress uniform. 'Won't you be seated?' The beds being up, there was room for a couple of folding armchairs. 'I'll send after coffee.'

'How did it go?' she asked, sitting down opposite him, nervously trying to make conversation. 'Did Malcolm attend?'

'Not today. I suspect our friend Foxe-Jameson is not yet sure whether he wants to return to the faith of his fathers or stay a loyal agnostic.' Telander smiled a bit. 'He'll come, though, he'll come. He simply needs to get it through his head that it's possible to be a Christian and an astrophysicist. When are we going to lure you, Ingrid?'

'Probably never. If there is any directing intelligence behind reality – and we've no scientific evidence in favor of that – why should it care about a chemical accident like man?'

'You quote Charles Reymont almost precisely, did you

know?' Telander said. Her features tensed. He hurried on: 'A being that concerns itself with everything from quanta to quasars can spare attention for us. Rational proof – But I don't want to repeat stale arguments. We've something else on hand.' He tuned his intercom to the galley: 'A pot of coffee, cream and sugar, two cups, in the captain's cabin, please.'

'Cream!' Lindgren muttered.

'I don't think our food technicians fake it badly,' Telander said. 'By the way, Carducci is quite taken with Reymont's suggestion.'

'What's that?'

'Working with the food team to invent new dishes. Not a beefsteak put together out of algae and tissue cultures, but stuff never experienced before. I'm glad he's found an interest.'

'Yes, as a chef he's been slipping.' Lindgren's garb of casualness fell off. She struck her chair arm. 'Why?' burst from her. 'What's wrong? We've been under weigh scarcely half as long as we planned on. Morale shouldn't rot this soon.'

'We've lost every assurance – '

'I know, I know. And shouldn't people be stimulated by danger? As for the chance we won't ever end our voyage, well, it hit me badly too, I admit, at first. But I think I've rallied.'

'You and I have an ongoing purpose,' Telander said. 'We, the regular crew, we're responsible for lives. It helps. And even for us – ' He paused. 'This is what I wished to talk over with you, Ingrid. We're at a critical date. The hundred-year mark on Earth since we departed.'

'Nonsensical,' she said. 'You can't speak of simultaneity under these conditions.'

'It's far from psychologically nonsensical,' he answered. 'At Beta Virginis we would have had a thread of contact with home. We would have thought that the younger ones we left behind, given longevity treatments, were still alive. If we must return, surely enough continuity would have persisted that we didn't come back as utter aliens. Now

93

though – the fact that in some sense, whether a mathematical one or not – at best, babies whom we saw in their cribs are nearing the end of life – it reminds us too hard, we can never regain any trace of what we once loved.'

'M-m-m . . . I suppose. Like watching somebody you care about die of a slow disease. You aren't surprised when the end comes; nevertheless, it is the end.' Lindgren blinked. 'Damn!'

'You must do what you can to help them through this period,' Telander said. 'You know how better than I.'

'You could do a good deal yourself.'

The gaunt head shook. 'Best not. On the contrary, I'm going to withdraw.'

'What do you mean?' she asked with a touch of alarm.

'Nothing dramatic,' he said. 'My work with the engineering and navigation departments, in these unpredictable circumstances, does take most of my waking hours. It'll provide a cover for my gradually ceasing to mix in shipboard society.'

'Whatever for?'

'I've had several talks with Charles Reymont. He has made an excellent point – a crucial one, I do believe. When uncertainty surrounds us, when despair is always waiting to break us . . . the average person aboard has to feel his life is in competent hands. Of course, no one is going to suppose consciously that the captain is infallible. But there's an unconscious need for such an aura. And I – I have my share of weakness and stupidity. My human-level judgments can't stand up to daily testing under high stress.'

Lindgren crouched in her seat. 'What does the constable want of you?'

'That I stop operating on an informal, intimate basis. The excuse will be that I mustn't be distracted by ordinary business, when my whole attention must go to getting us safely through the galaxy's clouds and clusters. It's a reasonable excuse, it will be accepted. In the end, I shall be dining separately, in here, except on ceremonial occasions. I shall take my exercise and recreation here too, alone. What personal visitors I have will be the highest-ranking officers, like you. We will surround me with official etiquette. Through his own assistants, Reymont will pass the word that polite forms of address toward me are expected of everyone.

'In short, your good gray friend Lars Telander is about to change into the Old Man.'

'It sounds like Reymont's kind of scheme,' she said bitterly.

'He's convinced me it's desirable,' the captain replied.

'With no thought for what it can do to you!'

'I'll manage. I never was hail-fellow-well-met. We have many books along in the microtapes that I always wanted to read.' Telander regarded her earnestly. Though the air was nearing the warmest part of its cycle and was tinged with a smell like new-mown hay, the fine hairs were standing erect on her arms. 'You have a role also, Ingrid. More than ever, you will handle the human problems. Organization, mediation, alleviation . . . it won't be easy.'

'I can't do it alone.' Her words wavered.

'You can if you must,' he told her. 'In practice you can delegate or divert much. That's a question of proper planning. We'll work it out as we go.'

He hesitated. Uneasiness came upon him; color actually entered his cheeks. 'Ah . . . a matter in that connection – '

'Yes?' she said.

The door chime rescued him. He accepted the coffee tray from the bull cook and made a performance of carrying it to his desk and pouring. It enabled him to keep his back to her.

'In your position,' he said. 'That is, your new position. The necessity of giving officers a special status – You needn't hold aloof like me, entirely – but a certain limitation of, well, accessibility – '

He couldn't see if it was actual amusement coloring her voice. 'Poor Lars! You mean the first officer should not change boy friends so often, don't you?'

'Well, I don't suggest, ah, celibacy. I myself must, of course, ah, hold back from such things hereafter. In your case – well, the experimental phase is past for most of us.

Stable relationships are forming. If you could make one – '

'I can do better,' she said. 'I can turn solitary.'

He could delay no further handing her a cup. 'Th-that isn't required,' he stammered.

'Thanks.' She inhaled the coffee's fragrance. Her eyes crinkled at him over the rim. 'We don't have to be absolutely abbot and nun, we two. The captain needs a private conference once in a while with his first officer.'

'Er – no. You are sweet, Ingrid, but no.' Telander paced the narrow width of the cabin, back and forth. 'In as little and cramped a community as this, how long can any secret last? I dare not risk hypocrisy. And while I . . . I would love to have you for a permanent partner . . . it can't be. You have to be everyone else's liaison with me: not my, my direct collaborator. Do you follow me? Reymont explained it better.'

Her humor died. 'I don't altogether like the way he's jockeyed you.'

'He's had experience in crisis situations. His arguments were sound. We can go over them in detail.'

'We will. They might be logical at that . . . whatever his motives.' Lindgren took a sip of coffee, set the cup down on her lap, and declared in a whetted voice:

'Regarding myself, all right. I'm tired of the whole childish business anyway. You're correct, monogamy is becoming fashionable, and a girl's choices are poxy limited. I've already considered stopping. Olga Sobieski feels the same. I'll tell Kato to trade cabin halves with her. Some calm and coolness will be welcome, Lars, a chance to think about several things, now that we really have gone by that hundred-year mark.'

Leonora Christine was aimed well away from the Virgin, but not yet at the Archer. Only after she had swung almost halfway around the galaxy would the majestic spiral of her path strike toward its heart. At present the Sagittarian nebulae stood off her port bow. What lay beyond them was inferred, not known. Astronomers expected a volume of clear space, with scant dust or gas, housing a crowded population of ancient stars. But no telescope had seen past the clouds which surrounded that realm, and no one had yet gone to look.

'Unless an expedition went off since we left,' pilot Lenkei suggested. 'It's been centuries on Earth. I imagine they're doing marvelous things.'

'Not dispatching probes to the core, surely,' cosmologist Chidambaran objected. 'Thirty millennia to get there, and as much to flash a message back? It does not make sense. I expect man will spread slowly inward, colony by colony.'

'Failing a faster-than-light drive,' Lenkei said.

Chidambaran's swarthy features and small-boned body came as near registering scorn as had ever been seen on him. 'That fantasy! If you want to rewrite everything we have learned since Einstein – no, since Aristotle, considering the logical contradiction involved in a signal without a limiting velocity – proceed.'

'Not my line of work.' Lenkei's greyhound slenderness seemed abruptly haggard. 'I don't want faster-than-light, anyhow. The idea that others might be speeding from star to star like birds – like me from town to town when I was home – while we're caged here . . . that would be too cruel.'

'Our fate would not be changed by their fortune,' Chidambaran replied. 'Indeed, irony would add another dimension to it, another challenge if you will.'

'I've more challenge than I want,' Lenkei said.

Their footfalls resounded on the winding stairs and up the well. They had come together from a low-level shop where Nilsson had been consulting Foxe-Jameson and Chidambaran about the design of a large crystal diffraction grating.

'It's easier for you,' exploded from the pilot. 'You've got a real use. We depend on your team. If you can't produce new instruments for us – Me, till we reach a planet where they need space ferries and aircraft, what am I?'

'You are helping build those instruments, or will be when we have plans drawn up,' Chidambaran said.

'Yes, I apprenticed myself to Sadek. To pass this bloody empty time.' Lenkei collected his wits. 'I'm sorry. An attitude we've got to steer clear of, I know. Mohandas, may I ask you something?'

'Certainly.'

'Why did you sign on? You're important today. But if we hadn't had the accident – couldn't you have gone further toward understanding the universe back on Earth? You're a theoretician, I'm told. Why not leave the fact gathering to men like Nilsson?'

'I would scarcely have lived to do much with reports from Beta Virginis. It seemed of possible value that a scientist of my sort expose himself to wholly new experiences and impressions. I might have gained insights that would never come otherwise. If I didn't, the loss would not be large, and at a minimum I would have continued thinking approximately as well as at home.'

Lenkei tugged his chin. 'Do you know,' he said, 'I suspect you don't need dream-box sessions.'

'It may be. I confess I find the process undignified.'

'Then for heaven's sake, why?'

'Regulations. We must all receive the treatment. I did request exemption. Constable Reymont persuaded First Officer Lindgren that special privilege, albeit justified, would set a bad precedent.'

'Reymont! That bastard again!'

'He may be correct,' Chidambaran said. 'It does me no harm, unless one counts the interruption of a train of thought, and that happens too seldom to be a major handicap.'

'Huh! You're more patient than I'd be.'

'I suspect Reymont must force himself into the box,' Chidambaran remarked. 'He, too, goes as infrequently as allowed. Have you observed, similarly, that he will take a drink but will never get tipsy? I believe he is under a compulsion, arising perhaps from a buried fear, to stay in control.'

'He is that. Do you know what he said to me last week? I'd only borrowed some sheet copper, it'd have gone right back by way of the furnace and the rolling mill, soon as I was through with it, so I hadn't bothered to check it out. That bastard said – '

'Forget it,' Chidambaran advised. 'He had a point. We are not on a planet. Whatever we lose is lost for good. Best not to take chances; and surely we have time for bureaucratic procedures.' The entrance to commons appeared. 'Here we are.'

They headed toward the hypnotherapeutic room. 'I trust your experience will be pleasant, Matyas,' Chidambaran said.

'Me too.' Lenkei winced. 'I've had a few terrible nightmares in there.' Brightening: 'And a wild lot of fun!'

Stars grew scattered. *Leonora Christine* was not crossing from one spiral arm of the galaxy to another – not yet; she was just in a lane of comparative emptiness. For lack of much intake mass, her acceleration diminished. That condition was very temporary, so shrunken was her tau; a few hundred cosmic years. But for some time inboard, the viewscreens to starboard opened mainly on black night.

A number of the crew found it preferable to the eldritch shapes and colors blazing to port.

Another Covenant Day arrived. The ceremonies and the subsequent party were less forlorn than might have been expected. Shock and grief had gotten eroded by ordinariness. At present, the dominant mood was of defiance.

Not everybody attended. Elof Nilsson, for one, stayed in the cabin he and Jane Sadler shared. He spent a lengthy while making sketches and estimates for his exterior telescope. When his brain wearied, he dialed the library index for fiction. The novel he selected, at random out of thousands, proved absorbing. He hadn't finished it when she returned.

He raised eyes that were bloodshot with fatigue. Except for the scanner screen, the room was unlighted. She stood, big, gaudy, not altogether steady, in shadow.

'Good Lord!' he exclaimed. 'It's five in the morning!'

'Have you finally noticed?' She grinned. The whisky

haze around her reached his nostrils, together with a muskiness. He took a pinch of snuff, a luxury that occupied a large part of his baggage allowance.

'*I'm* not due at work in three hours,' he said.

'Nor I. I told my boss I wanted a week's leave. He agreed. He'd better. Who else has he got?'

'What attitude is that? Suppose others on whom the ship depends behaved thus.'

'Tetsuo Iwamoto . . . Iwamoto Tetsuo, really; Japanese put last name first, like Chinese . . . like Hungarians, did you know? – 'cept when they're being polite to us ignorant Westerners – ' Sadler captured her thought. 'He's a nice man to work for. He can manage a spell 'thout me. So why not?'

'Nevertheless – '

She lifted a finger. 'I will not be scolded, Elof. You hear? I've borne with that o-ver-com-pensated inferiority complex of yours more'n I should've. And a lot else. Thinking maybe the rest of you'd grow up to match that IQ of yours. Enough's enough. Gather ye roses while ye may.'

'You're drunk.'

'Sort of.' Wistfully: 'You should've come along.'

'What for? Why not confess how weary I am of the same faces, the same actions, the same inane conversations? I'm far from unique in that.'

Her voice dropped. 'Are you tired of me?'

'Why – ' Nilsson's Kewpie-doll form clambered erect. 'What's the matter, my dear?'

'You haven't exactly bowled me over with attention, these past months.'

'No? No, perhaps not.' He drummed a dresser top. 'I've been preoccupied.'

She drew a breath. 'I'll say it straight. I was with Johann tonight.'

'Freiwald? The machinist?' Nilsson stood speechless for a humming minute. She waited. Soberness had come upon her. He said at length, with difficulty, watching the tattoo of his fingers: 'Well, you have the legal and doubtless the moral right. I am no handsome young animal. I am . . .

was . . . more proud and happy than I knew how to express when you agreed to be my partner. I let you teach me a number of things I did not understand before. Probably I was not the most adept pupil anyone ever had.'

'Oh, Elof!'

'You are leaving me, aren't you?'

'We're in love, he and I.' Her vision blurred. 'I thought it'd be easier than this to tell you. I didn't figure you cared a lot.'

'You wouldn't consider a discreet – No, discretion isn't feasible. Besides, you couldn't bring yourself to it. And I have my own pride.' Nilsson sat down again and reached for his snuffbox. 'You had better go. You can remove your things later.'

'That quick?'

'Get out!' he shrieked.

She fled, weeping but on eager feet.

Leonora Christine re-entered populated country. Passing within fifty light-years of a giant new-born sun, she transited the gas envelope that surrounded it. Being ionized, the atoms were seizable with maximum efficiency. Her tau plummeted close to asymptotic zero: and with it, her time rate.

CHAPTER 12

Reymont paused at the entrance to commons. The deck lay empty and quiet. After an initial surge of interest, athletics and other hobbies had become increasingly less popular. Aside from meals, the tendency was for scientists and crewfolk to form minute cliques or retreat altogether into reading, watching taped shows, sleeping as much as possible. He could force them to get a prescribed amount of exercise. But he had not found a way to restore what the months were grinding out of the spirit. He was the more helpless in that respect because his inflexible enforcement of basic rules had made him enemies.

A propos rules – He strode down the corridor to the dream room and opened its door. A light above each of the three boxes within said it was occupied. He fished a master key from his pocket and unlocked the lids, which passed air but not light, one by one. Two he closed again. At the third, he swore. The stretched-out body, the face under the somnohelmet, belonged to Emma Glassgold.

For a space he stood looking down at the small woman. Peace dwelt in her smile. Doubtless she, like most aboard, owed her continued sanity to this apparatus. Despite every effort at decoration, at actual interior construction of desired facilities, the ship was too sterile an environment. Total sensory deprivation quickly causes the human mind to lose its hold on reality. Deprived of the data-flow with which it is meant to deal, the brain spews forth hallucinations, goes irrational, and finally collapses into lunacy. The effects of prolonged sensory impoverishment are slower, subtler, but in many ways more destructive. Direct electronic stimulation of the appropriate encephalic centers becomes necessary. That is speaking in neurological terms. In terms of immediate emotion, the extraordinarily intense and lengthy dreams generated by the stimulus – whether pleasurable or not – become a substitute for real experience.

Nevertheless . . . .

Glassgold's skin was loose and unhealthy in hue. The EEG screen behind the helmet said she was in a soothed condition. That meant she could be roused fast without danger. Reymont snapped down the override switch on the timer. The oscilloscopic trace of the inductive pulses that had been going through her head flattened and darkened.

She stirred. '*Shalom*, Moshe,' he heard her whisper. There was nobody along of that name. He slid the helmet off. She squeezed her eyes tighter shut, knuckled them, and tried to turn around on the padding.

'Wake up.' Reymont gave her a shake.

She blinked at him. The breath snapped into her. She sat straight. He could almost see the dream fade away behind those eyes. 'Come on,' he said, offering his hand to assist. 'Out of that damned coffin.'

'Ach, no, no,' she slurred. 'I was with Moshe.'

'I'm sorry, but – '

She crumpled into sobbing. Reymont slapped the box, a crack across the ship's murmur. 'All right,' he said. 'I'll make that a direct order. Out! And report to Dr Latvala.'

'What the devil's going on here?'

Reymont turned. Norbert Williams must have heard them, the door being ajar, and come in from the pool, because the chemist was nude and wet. He was also furious. 'You've gotten to bullying women, huh?' he said. 'Not even big women. Scram.'

Reymont stood where he was. 'We have regulations about these boxes,' he said. 'If a person hasn't the self-discipline to obey them, I have to compel.'

'Yah! Snooping, peering, shoving your nose up our privacy – by God, I'm not going to stand for it any longer!'

'Don't,' Glassgold implored. 'Don't fight. I'm sorry. I will go.'

'Like hell you will,' the American answered. 'Stay. Insist on your rights.' His features burned crimson. 'I've had a bellyful of this little tin Jesus, and now's the time to do something about him.'

Reymont said, spacing his words: 'The regulation limiting use wasn't written for fun, Dr Williams. Too much is worse than none. It becomes addictive. The end result is insanity.'

'Listen.' The chemist made an obvious effort to curb his wrath. 'People aren't identical. *You* may think we can be stretched and trimmed to fit your pattern – you and your dragooning us into calisthenics, your arranging work details that a baby could see aren't for anything except to keep us busy a few hours a day, your smashing the still that Pedro Barrios built – your whole petty dictatorship, ever since we veered off on this Flying Dutchman chase – ' He lowered his volume. 'Listen,' he said. 'Those regulations. Like here. They're written to make sure nobody gets an overdose. Of course. But how do you know that some of us are getting enough? We've all got to spend time in the boxes. You too, Constable Iron Man. You too.'

'Certainly – ' Reymont was interrupted:

'How can you tell how much another guy may need? You don't have the sensitivity God gave a cockroach. Do you know one mucking thing about Emma? I do. I know she's a fine, courageous woman . . . perfectly well able to judge her own necessities and guide herself . . . she doesn't need you to run her life for her.' Williams pointed. 'There's the door. Use it.'

'Norbert, don't.' Glassgold climbed from the casket and tried to go between the men. Reymont eased her aside and answered Williams:

'If exceptions are to be made, the ship's physician is the person to determine them. Not you. She has to see Dr Latvala anyway, after this. She can ask him for a medical authorization.'

'I know how far she'll get with him. That louse won't even issue tranquilizers.'

'We've years ahead of us. Unforeseeable troubles to outlive. If we start getting dependent on pacifiers – '

'Did you ever think without some such help, we'll go crazy and die? We'll decide for ourselves, thank you. Get out, I said!'

Glassgold sought again to intervene. Reymont had to seize her by the arms to move her.

'*Take your hands off her, you swine!*' Williams charged with both fists flailing.

Reymont released Glassgold and drifted back, into the hall where room for maneuvering was available. Williams yelped and followed. Reymont guarded himself against the inexpert blows until, after a minute, he sprang. A karate flurry and two strokes sent Williams to the deck. He huddled, retching. Blood dripped from his nose.

Glassgold wailed and ran to him. She knelt, pulled him close, glared up at Reymont. 'Aren't you brave?' she spat.

The constable spread his palms. 'Was I supposed to let him hit me?'

'You c-c-could have left.'

'Impossible. My duty is to maintain order on board. Until Captain Telander relieves me, I'll continue to do so.'

'Very well,' Glassgold said between her teeth. 'We are going to him. I am lodging a formal complaint.'

Reymont shook his head. 'It was explained and agreed on when this situation developed, the skipper mustn't be bothered with our bickerings. He has to think of the ship.'

Williams groaned his way back toward full consciousness.

'We will see First Officer Lindgren,' Reymont said. 'I have to file charges against both of you.'

Glassgold compressed her lips. 'As you wish.'

'Not Lin'gren,' Williams mouthed. 'Lin'gren an' him, they was – '

'No longer,' Glassgold said. 'She couldn't stand any more of him, even before the accident. She will be fair.' With her help, Williams got dressed and limped to the command deck.

Several people saw the group pass and started to ask what had happened. Reymont snapped them into silence. The looks they returned were sullen. At the first intercom call box, he dialed Lindgren and requested her to be in the interview room.

It was minuscule but soundproof, a place for confidential hearings and necessary humiliations. Lindgren sat behind the desk. She had donned a uniform. The fluoropanel spilled light onto her frost-blond hair; the voice in which she bade Reymont commence, after they were all seated, was equally cold.

He gave a terse account of the incident. 'I charge Dr Glassgold with violation of a hygienic rule,' he finished, 'and Dr Williams with assault on a peace officer.'

'Mutiny?' Lindgren inquired. Dismay sprang forth on Williams.

'No, madame. Assault will suffice,' Reymont said. To the chemist: 'Consider yourself lucky. We can't psychologically afford a trial, which a charge of mutiny would bring. Not unless you persist in this kind of behavior.'

'That will do, Constable,' Lindgren clipped. 'Dr. Glassgold, will you give me your version?'

Anger still upbore the biologist. 'I plead guilty to the violation as alleged,' she declared firmly. 'but I am asking for a review of my case – of everybody's case – as provided by the articles. Not Dr Latvala's sole judgment; a board of officers and my colleagues. As for the fight, Norbert was intolerably provoked, and he was made the victim of sheer viciousness.'

'Your statement, Dr Williams?'

'I don't know how I stand under your fool reg -- ' The American checked himself. 'Pardon me, ma'm,' he said, a trifle thickly through his puffed lips. 'I never did memorize space law. I thought common sense and good will would see us through. Reymont may be technically in the right, but I've had about my limit of his brass-headed interference.'

'Then, Dr Glassgold, Dr Williams, are you willing to abide by my sentence? You are entitled to a trial if you desire it.'

Williams achieved a lopsided smile. 'Matters are bad enough already, ma'm. I suppose this has to go in the log, but maybe it doesn't have to go in the whole crew's ears.'

'Oh yes,' Glassgold breathed. She caught Williams' hand.

Reymont opened his mouth. 'You are under my authority, Constable,' Lindgren intercepted him. 'You may, of course, appeal to the captain.'

'No, madame,' Reymont answered.

'Well, then.' Lindgren leaned back. Her countenance thawed. 'I order accusations on every side of this case dropped – or, rather, never be filed. This is not to be entered on any record. Let us talk the problem out as among human beings who are all in, shall I say, the same boat.'

'Him too?' Williams jerked a thumb at Reymont.

'We must have law and discipline, you know,' Lindgren said mildly. 'Without them, we die. Perhaps Constable

Reymont gets overzealous. Or perhaps not. In any event, he is the single police and military specialist we have. If you dissent from him . . . that's what I'm here for. Do relax. I'll send for coffee.'

'If the first officer pleases,' Reymont said, 'I'll excuse myself.'

'No, we have things to say to you,' Glassgold snapped.

Reymont kept his eyes on Lindgren's. It was as if sparks flew between. 'As you explained, madame,' he said, 'my job is to preserve the rules of the ship. No more, no less. This has become something else: a personal counseling session. I'm sure the lady and gentleman will talk easier without me.'

'I believe you are right, Constable.' She nodded. 'Dismissed.'

He rose, saluted, and left. On his way upstairs he encountered Freiwald, who greeted him. He had kept some approximation of cordiality with his half dozen deputies.

He entered his cabin. The beds were down, joined into one. Chi-Yuen sat on it. She wore a light, frilly peignoir which made her resemble a little girl, a sad one. 'Hello,' she said tonelessly. 'You have thunder in your face. What happened?'

Reymont settled beside her and related it.

'Well,' she asked, 'can you blame them very much?'

'No. I suppose not. Though – I don't know. This band was intended to be the best Earth could offer. Intelligence, education, stable personality, health, dedication. And they knew they'd likely never come home again. At a minimum, they'd return to countries older than the ones they left by the better part of a century.' Reymont ran fingers through his wire-brush hair. 'So things have changed,' he sighed. 'We're off to an unknown destiny, maybe to death, certainly to complete isolation. But is it that different from what we were planning on from the start? Should it make us go to pieces?'

'It does,' Chi-Yuen said.

'You too. I've been meaning to take that up with you.' He gave her a ferocious look. 'You were busy at first, your amusements, your theoretical work, your programming the studies you wanted to carry out in the Beta Vee System. And when the trouble hit us, you responded well.'

A ghostly smile crossed her. She patted his cheek. 'You inspired me.'

'Since then, however . . . more and more, you sit doing nothing. We had the beginnings of something real, you and I; but you don't often make meaningful contact with me of late. You're seldom interested in talk or sex or anything, including other people. No more work. No more big day-dreams. Not even crying into your pillow after lights out . . . oh yes, I'd lie awake and hear you. Why, Ai-Ling? What's happening to you? To them?'

'I imagine we have not quite your raw will to survive at any cost,' she said, almost inaudibly.

'I'd consider some prices for life too high myself. Here, though – We have what we need. A certain amount of comfort to boot. An adventure like nothing ever before. What's wrong?'

'Do you know what the year is on Earth?' she countered.

'No. I was the one who got Captain Telander to order that particular clock removed. Too morbid an attitude was developing around it.'

'Most of us can make our own estimates anyway.' She spoke in a level, indifferent voice. 'At present, I believe it is about anno Domini 10,000 at home. Give or take several centuries. And yes, I learned in school about the concept of simultaneity breaking down under relativistic conditions. And I remember that the century mark was expected to be the great psychological hurdle. In spite of that, these mounting dates have meaning. They make us absolute exiles. Already. Irrevocably. No longer simply our kinfolk must be extinct. Our civilization must be. What has happened on Earth? Throughout the galaxy? What have men done? What have they become? We will never share in it. We cannot.'

He tried to break her apathy with sharpness: 'What of that? On Beta Three, the maser would have brought us words a generation old. Nothing else. And our individual deaths would have closed us off from the universe. The common fate of man. Why should we whine if ours takes an unexpected shape?'

She regarded him gravely before she told him, 'You don't really want an answer for yourself. You want to pull one out of me.'

Startled, he said, 'Well . . . yes.'

'You understand people better than you let on. Your business, no doubt. You tell me what our trouble is.'

'Loss of control over life,' he replied at once. 'The crew aren't in such bad condition yet. They have their jobs. But the scientists, like you, had vowed themselves to Beta Virginis. They had heroic, exciting work to look forward to, and meanwhile their preparations to make. Now they've no idea what will happen. They know just that it'll be something altogether unpredictable. That it may be death – because we are taking frightful risks – and they can do nothing to help, only sit passive and be carried. Of course their morale cracks.'

'What do you think we should do, Charles?'

'Well, in your case, for instance, why not continue your work? Eventually we'll be searching for a world to settle on. Planetology will be vital to us.'

'You're aware what the odds are against that. We are going to keep on this devil's hunt until we die.'

'Damnation, we can improve the odds!'

'How?'

'That's one of the things you ought to be working on.'

She smiled again, a little more alive. 'Charles, you make me want to. If for no other reason than to make you stop flogging at me. Is that why you are so tough with the others?'

He considered her. 'You've borne up better than most thus far,' he said. 'It might help you get back your purpose if I share what I'm doing with you. Can you keep a trade secret?'

Her glance actually danced. 'You should know me that well by now.' One bare foot rubbed across his thigh.

He patted it and chuckled. 'An old principle,' he said. 'Works in military and paramilitary organizations. I've been applying it here. The human animal wants a father-mother image but, at the same time, resents being disciplined. You can get stability like this: The ultimate authority-source is kept remote, godlike, practically unapproachable. Your immediate superior is a mean son of a bitch who makes you toe the mark and whom you therefore detest. But his own superior is as kind and sympathetic as rank allows. Do you follow me?'

She laid a finger to her temple. 'Not really.'

'Take our present situation. You'd never guess how I juggled, those first few months after we hit the nebulina. I don't claim credit for the whole development. A lot of it was natural, almost inevitable. The logic of our problem brought it about, given some nursing by me. The end result is that Captain Telander's been isolated. His infallibility doesn't have to cope with essentially unfixable human messes like the one today.'

'Poor man.' Chi-Yuen looked closely at Reymont. 'Lindgren is his surrogate for those?'

He nodded. 'I'm the traditional top sergeant. Hard, harsh, demanding, overbearing, inconsiderate, brutal. Not so bad as to start a petition for my removal. But enough to irritate, to be disliked, although respected. That's good for the troops. It's healthier to be mad at me than to dwell on personal woes . . . as you, my love, have been doing.

'Lindgren smooths things out. As first officer, she sustains my power. But she overrules me from time to time. She exercises her rank to bend regulations in favor of mercy. Therefore she adds benignity to the attributes of Ultimate Authority.'

Reymont frowned. 'The system's carried us this far,' he finished. 'It's beginning to fail. We'll have to add a new factor.'

Chi-Yuen went on gazing at him until he shifted uncomfortably on the mattress. At last she asked, 'Did you plan this with Ingrid?'

'Eh? Oh no. Her role demands she *not* be a Machiavelli type who'd play a part deliberately.'

'You understand her so well . . . from past acquaintance?'

'Yes.' He reddened. 'What of it? These days we keep it purely formal. For obvious reasons.'

'I think you find ways to continue rebuffing her, Charles.'

'M-m-m . . . blast it, leave me alone. What I'm trying to do is help you get back some real wish to live.'

'So that I, in turn, can help you keep going?'

'Well, uh, yes. I'm no superman. It's been too long since anybody lent me a shoulder to cry on.'

'Are you saying that because you mean it, or because it serves your purpose?' Chi-Yuen tossed back her locks. 'Never mind. Don't answer. We will do what we can for each other. Afterward, if we survive – We will settle that when we have survived.'

His dark, scarred features softened. 'You are for a fact regaining your balance,' he said. 'Excellent.'

She laughed. Her arms went about his neck. 'Come here, you.'

CHAPTER 13

The speed of light can be approached, but no body possessing rest mass can quite attain it. Smaller and smaller grew the increments of velocity by which *Leonora Christine* neared that impossible ultimate. Thus it might have seemed that the universe which her crew observed could not be distorted further. Aberration could, at most, displace a star $45°$; Doppler effect might infinitely redden the photons from astern but only double the frequencies from ahead.

However, there was no limit on inverse tau, and that was the measure of changes in perceived space and experienced time. Accordingly, there was no limit to optical changes either; and the cosmos fore and aft could shrink toward a zero thickness wherein all the galaxies were crowded.

Thus, as she made her great swing half around the Milky

Way and turned for a plunge through its heart, the ship's periscope revealed a weird demesne. The nearer stars streamed past ever faster, until at last the eye saw them marching across the field of view: because by that time, years went by outside while minutes ticked away within. The sky was no longer black; it was a shimmering purple, which deepened and brightened as interior months went by: because the interaction of force fields and interstellar medium – eventually, interstellar magnetism – was releasing quanta. The farther stars were coalescing into two globes, fiery blue ahead, deep crimson aft. But gradually those globes contracted toward points and dimmed: because well-nigh the whole of their radiation had been shifted out of the visible spectrum, toward gamma rays and radio waves.

The viewscope had been repaired but was increasingly less able to compensate. The circuits simply could not distinguish individual suns any longer at more than a few parsecs' remove. The technicians took the instrument apart and rebuilt it for heightened capacity, lest men fly altogether sightless.

That project, and various other remodelings, were probably of more use to those able to do the work than they were in themselves. Such persons did not withdraw into their own shells as did too many of their shipmates.

Boris Fedoroff found Luis Pereira on the hydroponics deck. An alga tank was being harvested. The biosystems chief worked with his men, stripped like them, dripping the same water and green slime, filling the crocks that stood on a cart. 'Phew!' said the engineer.

Teeth gleamed under Pereira's mustache. 'Do not deprecate my crop that loudly,' he replied. 'You will be eating it in due course.'

'I wondered how the imitation Limburger cheese got so realistic,' Fedoroff said. 'Can you come for a discussion with me?'

'Could it not be later? We can't stop until we are through. If spoilage set in, you would be tightening your belt for a while.'

'I don't have time to waste either,' Fedoroff said, turning astringent. 'I believe we'd rather be hungry than wrecked.'

'Carry on, then,' Pereira told his gang. He hopped from the tank and went to a shower stall where he washed quickly. Not bothering to dry or dress himself, on this warmest level in the ship, he led Fedoroff toward his office. 'Confidentially,' he admitted, 'I'm delighted at an excuse to knock off that chore.'

'You will be less delighted when you hear the reason. It means hard work.'

'Better yet. I was wondering how to keep my team from coming apart. This isn't the sort of occupation that generates spontaneous *esprit de corps*. The boys will grumble, but they will be happier with something besides routine.'

They passed through a section of green plants. Leaves lined every passageway, filling the air with odor, rustling when brushed. Fruits hung among them like lanterns. You could understand why a degree of serenity remained in those who labored here.

'I've been alerted by Foxe-Jameson,' Fedoroff explained. 'We're near enough to the central galactic nebulae that he can use the new instruments that have been developed to get accurate values for the mass densities there.'

'He? I thought Nilsson was the observations man.'

'He was supposed to be.' Fedoroff's mouth set in hard lines. 'He's going to pot. Hasn't contributed a thing lately except quibbles and quarrels. The rest of his group, even a couple of men from the shop making their stuff, like Lenkei... they have to do what he should, as best they can.'

'That is bad,' Pereira said, lighthearted no more. 'We were relying on Nilsson to design instruments for intergalactic navigation at ultra-low tau, were we not?'

Fedoroff nodded. 'He'd better pull out of his funk. But that isn't the problem today. We're going to encounter the thickest stretch so far when we hit those clouds, because of relativity and because they are in fact thick. I feel reasonably confident we can pass through safely. Nevertheless, I want to reinforce parts of the hull to make sure.' He laughed like a wolf. ' "Make sure" – on such a flight! At any rate, I'll have a construction gang in here. You'll have to move installations out of their way. I want to discuss the general requirements with you and start you thinking, so you can plan how to minimize the disturbance to your operations.'

'Indeed. Indeed. Here we are.' Pereira waved Fedoroff into a cubbyhole with a desk and filing cabinet. 'I will show you a schematic of our layout.'

They talked business for half an hour. (Centuries passed beyond the hull.) The trace of geniality he had shown at first, which was once the usual face he turned to the world, had vanished from Fedoroff. He was short-spoken to the point of rudeness.

When he had stowed the drawings and notes, Pereira said quietly: 'You do not sleep well these nights, do you?'

'Busy,' the engineer grunted.

'Old friend, you thrive on work. That is not what drew those smudges beneath your eyes. It is Margarita, no?'

Fedoroff jerked in his chair. 'What about her?' He and Jimenes had lived steadily together for several months.

'In our village, no one can help noticing she has a grief.'

Fedoroff stared out the entrance, into the greenness. 'I wish I could leave her without feeling like a deserter,' he said.

'M-m-m . . . you recall I was often with her before she settled down. Perhaps I have an insight you don't. You are not insensitive, Boris, but you seldom resonate with the feminine mind. I wish you two well. Can I help?'

'The thing is, she refuses to take antisenescence. Neither Urho Latvala nor I can budge her. No doubt I tried too hard and made her think I was browbeating. She'll scarcely speak to me.' Fedoroff's tone harshened. He continued to watch the leaves outside. 'I was never in love . . . with her. Nor she with me. But we became fond. I want to do anything I can for her. What, though?'

'She is a young woman,' Pereira said. 'If our circumstances have made her, how shall I put it, overwrought, she might react irrationally to any reminder of age and death.'

Fedoroff swung about. 'She's not ignorant! She's perfectly

aware the treatment has to be periodic through a whole adulthood – or menopause will hit her fifty years before it needs to. She says that's what she wants!'

'Why?'

'She wants to be dead before the chemical and ecological systems break down. You predicted five decades for that, didn't you?'

'Yes. A slow, nasty way to go out. If we haven't found a planet by then – '

'She remains Christian. Prejudices about suicide.' Fedoroff winced. 'I don't like the prospect either. Who does? She won't believe it isn't inevitable.'

'I suspect,' Pereira said, 'the idea of dying childless is to her the true horror. She used to make a game of deciding on names for the large family she wants.'

'Do you mean – Wait. Let me think. Damn him, Nilsson was right the other day, about the unlikelihood of our ever finding a home. I have to agree, life in that case seems pretty futile.'

'To her especially. Facing that emptiness, she retreats – unconsciously, no doubt – toward a permissible form of suicide.'

'What can we *do*, Luis?' Fedoroff asked in anguish.

'If the captain was persuaded to make the treatments mandatory – He could justify that. Supposing we do reach a planet in spite of everything, the community will need each woman's childbearing span at a maximum.'

The engineer flared up. 'Another regulation? Reymont dragging her off to the doctor? No!'

'You should not hate Reymont,' Pereira reproached. 'You two are alike. Neither is a quitter.'

'Someday I'll kill him.'

'Now you display your romantic streak,' Pereira said, attempting to ease the atmosphere. 'He is pragmatism personified.'

'What would he do about Margarita, then?' Fedoroff gibed.

'Oh . . . I don't know. Something unsentimental. For instance, he might co-opt a research and development team to improve the biosystems and organocycles – make the ship indefinitely habitable – so she could be allowed two children, at least – '

His words trailed off. The men stared gape-mouthed at each other. It blazed between them:

Why not?

Maria Toomajian ran into the gym and found Johann Freiwald working out on the trapezes. 'Deputy!' she cried. Dismay shivered in her. 'At the game room, a fight!'

He bounced to the deck and pelted down the corridor. The noise reached him first, an excited babble. A dozen off-duty persons crowded in a circle. Freiwald shoved through. At the middle, second pilot Pedro Barrios and bull cook Michael O'Donnell panted and threw bare-knuckled blows. Slight harm had been done, but the sight was ugly.

'Stop that!' Freiwald bellowed.

They did, glaring. Folk had seen ere now the tricks that Reymont had drilled into his recruits. 'What is this farce?' Freiwald demanded. He turned his contempt on the watchers. 'Why didn't any of you take action? Are you too stupid to understand what this kind of behavior can lead to?'

'Nobody accuses me of cheating at cards,' O'Donnell said.

'You did,' Barrios retorted.

They lunged afresh. Freiwald's hands shot out. He got a grip on the collar of either tunic and twisted, pressing into the Adam's apples behind. The men flailed and kicked. He delivered a couple of *fumikomi*. They wheezed their pain and yielded.

'You could have used boxing gloves or kendo sticks in the ring,' Freiwald said. 'Now you're going before the first officer.'

'Er, pardon me.' A slim, dapper newcomer eased past the embarrassed witnesses and tapped Freiwald's shoulder: cartographer Phra Takh. 'I don't believe that's necessary.'

'Mind your own business,' Freiwald growled.

'It is my business,' Takh said. 'Our unity is essential to

116

our very lives. It won't be helped by official penalties. I am a friend of both these men. I believe I can mediate their disagreement.'

'We must have respect for the law, or we're done,' Freiwald replied. 'I'm taking them in.'

Takh reached a decision. 'May I talk privately with you first? For a minute?' His tone held urgency.

'Well . . . all right,' Freiwald agreed. 'You two stay here.'

He entered the game room with Takh and shut the door. 'I can't let them get away with resisting me,' he said. 'Ever since Captain Telander gave us deputies official status, we've acted for the ship.' Being clad in shorts, he lowered a sock to show the contusions on an ankle.

'You could ignore that,' Takh suggested. 'Pretend you didn't notice. They aren't bad fellows. They're simply driven wild by monotony, purposelessness, the tension of wondering if we will get through what's ahead of us or crash into a star.'

'If we let anybody escape the consequences of starting violence – '

'Suppose I took them aside. Suppose I got them to compose their differences and apologize to you. Wouldn't that serve the cause better than an arrest and a summary punishment?'

'It might,' Freiwald said skeptically. 'But why should I believe you can do it?'

'I am a deputy too,' Takh told him.

'What?' Freiwald goggled.

'Ask Reymont, when you can get him alone. I am not supposed to reveal that he recruited me, except to a regular deputy in an emergency situation. Which I judge this is.'

'*Aber* . . . why – ?'

'He meets a good deal of resentment, resistance, and evasion himself,' Takh said. 'His overt part-time agents, like you, have less trouble of that sort. You seldom have to do any dirty work. Still, a degree of opposition to you exists, and certainly no one will confide anything if he thinks Reymont might object. I am not a . . . a fink. We face no real crime problem. I am supposed to be a leaven, to the best of what abilities I have. As in this case today.'

'I thought you didn't like Reymont,' Freiwald said weakly.

'I cannot say I do,' Takh answered. 'Even so, he took me aside and convinced me I could perform a service for the ship. I assume you won't let out the secret.'

'Oh no. Certainly not. Not even to Jane. What a surprise!'

'Will you let me handle Pedro and Michael?'

'Yes, do.' Freiwald spoke absently. 'How many more of your kind are there?'

'I haven't the faintest idea,' Takh said, 'but I suspect that he hopes eventually to include everybody.' He went out.

CHAPTER 14

The nebular masses which walled in the galaxy's core loomed thunderhead black and betowered. Already *Leonora Christine* traversed their outer edge. No suns were visible forward; elsewhere, each hour, they shone fewer and fainter.

In this concentration of star stuff, she moved according to an eerie sort of aerodynamics. Her inverse tau was now so enormous that space density did not much trouble her. Rather, she swallowed matter still more greedily than before and was no longer confined to hydrogen atoms. Her readjusted selectors turned everything they met, gas or dust or meteoroids, into fuel and reaction mass. Her kinetic energy and time differential mounted at a dizzying rate. She flew as if through a wind blowing between the sun clusters.

Nonetheless, Reymont haled Nilsson to the interview room.

Ingrid Lindgren took her place behind its desk, in uniform. She had lost weight, and her eyes were shadowed. The cabin thrummed abnormally loud, and frequent shocks went through bulkheads and deck. The ship felt irregularities in the clouds as gusts, currents, vortices of an ongoing creation of worlds.

'Can this not wait till we have made our passage, Constable?' she asked, alike in anger and weariness.

'I don't think so, madame,' Reymont replied. 'Should an emergency arise, we need people convinced it's worth coping with.'

'You accuse Professor Nilsson of spreading disaffection. The articles provide for free speech.'

His chair creaked beneath the astronomer's shifting weight. 'I am a scientist,' he declared waspishly. 'I have not only the right but the obligation to state what is true.'

Lindgren regarded him with disfavor. He was letting a scraggly beard grow on his chins, had not bathed of late, and was in grimy coveralls.

'You don't have the right to spread horror stories,' Reymont said. 'Didn't you notice what you were doing to some of the women, especially, when you talked the way you did at mess? That's what decided me to intervene; but you'd been building up the trouble for quite a while before, Nilsson.'

'I merely brought out into the open what has been common knowledge from the start,' the fat man retorted. 'They hadn't the courage to discuss it in detail. I do.'

'They hadn't the meanness. You do.'

'No personalities,' Lindgren said. 'Tell me what happened.' She had recently been taking her meals alone in her cabin, pleading busyness, and was not seen much off watch.

'You know,' Nilsson said. 'We've raised the subject on occasion.'

'What subject?' she asked. 'We've talked about many.'

'Talked, yes, like reasonable people,' Reymont snapped. 'Not lectured a tableful of shipmates, most of them feeling low already.'

'Please, Constable. Proceed, Professor Nilsson.'

The astronomer puffed himself up. 'An elementary thing. I cannot comprehend why the rest of you have been such idiots as not to give it serious consideration. You blandly assume we will come to rest in a Virgo galaxy and find a habitable planet. But tell me how. Think of the require-, ments. Mass, temperature, irradiation, atmosphere, hydrosphere, biosphere . . . the best estimate is that 1 per cent of the stars may have planets which are any approximation to Earth.'

'That,' Lindgren said. 'Why, certainly – '

Nilsson was not to be deprived of his platform. Perhaps he didn't bother to hear her. He ticked points off on his fingers. 'If 1 per cent of the stars are suitable, do you realize how many we will have to examine in order to have an even chance of finding what we seek? Fifty! I should have thought anyone aboard would be capable of that calculation. It is conceivable that we will be lucky and come upon our Nova Terra at the first star we try. But the odds against this are ninety-nine to one. Doubtless we must try many. Now the examination of each involves almost a year of deceleration. To depart from it, in search elsewhere, requires another year of acceleration. Those are years of ship's time, remember, because nearly the whole period is spent at velocities which are small compared to light's and thus involve a tau factor near unity: which, in addition, prevents our going above one gravity.

'Hence we must allow a minimum of two years per star. The even chance of which I spoke – and mind you, it is only even – the odds are as good that we will not find Nova Terra in the first fifty stars as they are that we will – this chance requires a hundred years of search. Actually it requires more, because we shall have to stop from time to time and laboriously replenish the reaction mass for the ion drive. Antisenescence or no, we will not live that long.

'Therefore our whole endeavor, the risks we take in this fantastic dive straight through the galaxy and out into intergalactic space, it is all an exercise in futility. *Quod erat demonstrandum.*'

'Among your many loathsome characteristics, Nilsson,' Reymont said, 'is your habit of droning the obvious through your nose.'

'Madame!' the astronomer gasped. 'I protest! I shall file charges of personal abuse!'

'Cut back,' Lindgren ordered. 'Both of you. I must admit your conduct offers provocation, Professor Nilsson. On the other hand, Constable, may I remind you that Professor Nilsson is one of the most distinguished men in his vocation that Earth has . . . Earth had. He deserves respect.'

'Not the way he behaves,' Reymont said. 'Or smells.'

'Be polite, Constable, or I'll charge you myself.' Lindgren drew breath. 'You don't seem to make allowance for humanness. We are adrift in space and time; the world we knew is a hundred thousand years in its grave; we are rushing nearly blind into the most crowded part of the galaxy; we may at any minute strike something that will destroy us; at best, we must look forward to years in a cramped and barren environment. Don't you expect people to react to that?'

'Yes, madame, I do,' Reymont said. 'I do not expect them to behave so as to make matters worse.'

'There is some truth in that,' Lindgren conceded.

Nilsson squirmed and looked sulky. 'I was trying to spare them disappointment at the end of this flight,' he muttered.

'Are you absolutely certain you weren't indulging your ego?' Lindgren sighed. 'Never mind. Your standpoint is legitimate.'

'No, it isn't,' Reymont contradicted. 'He gets his 1 per cent by counting every star. But obviously we aren't going to bother with red dwarfs – the vast majority – or blue giants or anything outside a fairly narrow spectral range. Which reduces the field of search by a whopping factor.'

'Make the factor ten,' Nilsson said. 'I don't really believe that, but let's postulate we have a 10 per cent probability of finding Nova Terra at any one of the Sol-type stars we try. That nevertheless requires us to hunt among five to get our even chance. Ten years? More like twenty, all things considered. The youngest among us will be getting past his youth. The loss of so many reproductive opportunities means a corresponding loss of heredity; and our gene pool is minimal to start with. If we wait several decades to beget children, we can't beget enough. Few will be grown to self-sufficiency by the time their parents start becoming helpless with advancing age. And in any case, the human stock will die out in three or four generations. I know something about genetic drift, you see.'

His expression grew smug. 'I didn't wish to hurt feelings,' he said. 'My desire was to help, by showing your concept of a bold pioneer community, planting humankind afresh in a new galaxy . . . showing that for the infantile fantasy which it is.'

'Have you an alternative?' Lindgren inquired.

A tic began in Nilsson's face. 'Nothing but realism,' he said. 'Acceptance of the fact that we will never leave this ship. Adjustment of our behavior to that fact.'

'Is it the reason you've been soldiering on the job?' Reymont demanded.

'I dislike your term, sir, but it is true there is no point in building equipment for long-range navigation. We are not going anywhere that makes any difference. I cannot even get enthusiastic about Fedoroff's and Pereira's proposals concerning the life support systems.'

'You understand, I suppose,' Reymont said, 'that for maybe half the people aboard, the logical thing to do once they've decided you're right, is to commit suicide.'

'Possibly,' Nilsson shrugged.

'Do you hate life so much yourself?' Lindgren asked.

Nilsson half got up and fell down again. He gobbled. Reymont surprised both his listeners by turning soft-mannered:

'I didn't fetch you here only to get your gloom-peddling stopped. I'd rather know why you haven't been thinking how to improve our chances.'

'How can they be?'

'That's what I want to learn from you. You're the observational expert. As I recall, you were in charge of programs back home which located something like fifty planetary systems. You actually identified individual planets, and typed them, across light-years. Why can't you do the same for us?'

Nilsson pounced. 'Ridiculous! I see that I must explain the topic in kindergarten terms. Will you bear with me, First Officer? Pay attention, Constable.

'Granted, an extremely large space-borne instrument can pick out an object the size of Jupiter at a distance of several parsecs. This is provided the object gets good illumination without becoming lost in the glare of its sun. Granted, by mathematical analysis of perturbation data gathered over a period of years, some idea can be obtained about companion planets which are too small to photograph. Ambiguities in the equations can, to a degree, be resolved by close interferometric study of flare-type phenomena on the star; planets do exert a minor influence upon those cycles.

'But' – his finger prodded Reymont's chest – 'you do not realize how uncertain those results are. Journalists delighted in trumpeting that another Earthlike world had been discovered. The fact always was, however, that this was one possible interpretation of our data. Only one among numerous possible size and orbit distributions. And subject to a gross probable error. And this, mind you, with the largest, finest instruments which could be constructed. Instruments such as we do not have with us here, nor have room for if we could somehow build them.

'No, even at home, the sole way to get detailed information about extrasolar planets was to send a probe and later a manned expedition. In our case, the sole way is to decelerate for a close survey. And thereafter, I am convinced, to go on. Because you must be aware that a planet which otherwise seems ideal can be sterile or can have a native biochemistry that is useless or outright deadly to us.

'I implore you, Constable, to learn a little science, a little logic, and a bare touch of realism. Eh?' Nilsson ended with a crow of triumph.

'Professor – ' Lindgren tried.

Reymont smiled crookedly. 'Don't worry, madame,' he said. 'No fight will come of it. His words don't diminish me.'

He inspected the other man. 'Believe it or not,' he went on, 'I knew what you've told us. I also knew you are, or were, an able fellow. You made innovations, designed gadgets, that were responsible for a lot of discoveries. You were doing a fine job for us till you quit. Why not put your brain to work on the problems we have?'

'Will you be so good as to condescend to suggest a procedure?' Nilsson sneered.

'I'm no scientist, nor much of a technician,' Reymont said. 'Still, a few things look obvious to me. Let's suppose we have entered our target galaxy. We've shed the ultra-low tau we needed to get there, but we have one yet of . . . oh, whatever is convenient. Ten to the minus third, maybe? Well, that gives you a terrifically long baseline and cosmic-time period to make your observations. In the course of weeks or months, ship's time, you can collect more data on a given star than you had on any of Sol's neighbors. I should think you could find ways to use relativity effects to give you information that wasn't available at home. And naturally, you can observe a large number of Sol-type stars simultaneously. So you're bound to find some you can prove – prove with exact figures that leave no reasonable doubt – have planets with masses and orbits about like Earth's.'

'Assuming that, the question of atmosphere, biosphere, will remain. We need a short-range look.'

'Yes, yes. Must we stop to take it, though? Suppose, instead, we lay out a course which brings us hard by the most promising suns, in sequence, while we continue to travel near light-speed. In cosmic time, we'll have hours or days to check whatever planet interests us. Spectroscopic, thermoscopic, photographic, magnetic, write your own list of clues. We can get a fair idea of conditions on the surface. Biological conditions too. We could look for items like thermodynamic disequilibrium, chlorophyl-reflection spectra, polarization by microbe populations based on L-amino acids . . . yes, I imagine we can get an excellent notion of whether that planet is suitable. At low tau, we can examine any number in a small stretch of our own time. We'll have to use automation and electronics, in fact; we ourselves couldn't work fast enough. Then, when we've identified the right world, we can return to it. That will take a couple of years, agreed. But they'll be endurable years. We'll know, with high probability, that we have a home waiting for us.'

Color mounted in Lindgren's features. Her eyes grew less dull. 'Good Lord,' she said, 'why didn't you speak of this before?'

'I'd other problems on my mind,' Reymont answered. 'Why didn't you, Professor Nilsson?'

'Because the whole thing is absurd,' the astronomer snorted. 'You presuppose instrumentation we do not have.'

'Can't we build it? We have tools, precision equipment, construction supplies, skilled workmen. Your team has already made progress'

'You demand speed and sensitivity increased by whole orders of magnitude over anything that ever existed.'

'Well?' Reymont said.

Nilsson and Lindgren stared at him. The ship trembled.

'Well, why can't we develop what we need?' Reymont asked in a puzzled voice. 'We have some of the most talented, highly trained, imaginative people our civilization produced. They include every branch of science; what they don't know, they can find in the microtapes; they're used to interdisciplinary work.

'Suppose, for instance, Emma Glassgold and Norbert Williams got together to draw up the specifications for a device to detect and analyze life at a distance. They'd consult others as needed. Eventually they'd employ physicists, electronicians, and the rest for the actual building and debugging. Meanwhile, Professor Nilsson, you may have been in charge of a group making tools for remote planetography. In fact, you're the logical man to head up the entire program.'

Hardness fell from him. He exclaimed, eager as a boy: 'Why, this is precisely what we've needed! A fascinating, vital sort of job that demands everything everybody can give. Those whose specialties aren't called for, they'll be in it too – assistants, draftsmen, manual workers. . . . I suppose we'll have to remodel a cargo deck to accommodate the gear. . . .

Ingrid, it's a way to save not just our lives but our minds!'

He sprang to his feet. She did too. Their hands clasped.

Suddenly they became aware of Nilsson. He sat less than dwarfish, hunched, shivering, collapsed.

Lindgren went to him in alarm. 'What's wrong?'

His head did not lift. 'Impossible,' he mumbled. 'Impossible.'

'Surely not,' she urged. 'I mean, you wouldn't have to discover new laws of nature, would you? The basic principles are known.'

'They must be applied in unheard-of ways.' Nilsson covered his face. 'God better me, I haven't the brains any longer.'

Lindgren and Reymont exchanged a look above his bent back. She shaped unspoken words. Once he had taught her the Rescue Corps trick of lip reading when spacesuit radios were unusable. They had practiced it as something that made them more private and more one. *'Can we succeed without him?'*

'I doubt it. He is the best chief for that kind of project. At least, lacking him, our chance is poor.'

Lindgren squatted down beside Nilsson. She laid an arm across his shoulders. 'What's the trouble?' she asked most softly.

'I have no hope,' he snuffled. 'Nothing to live for.'

'You do!'

'You know Jane ... deserted me ... months ago. No other woman will – Why should I care? What's left for me?'

Reymont's lips formed, *'So behind everything was self-pity.'* Lindgren frowned and shook her head.

'No, you're mistaken, Elof,' she murmured. 'We do care for you. Would we ask for your help if we didn't honor you?'

'My mind.' He sat straight and glared at her out of swimming eyes. 'You want my intelligence, right. My advice. My knowledge and talent. To save yourselves. But do you want me? Do you think of me as, as a human being? No! Dirty old Nilsson. One is barely polite to him. When he starts to talk, one finds the earliest possible excuse to leave. One does not invite him to one's cabin parties. At most, if desperate, one asks him to be a fourth for bridge or to start an instrument development effort. What do you expect him to do? Thank you?'

'That isn't true!'

'Oh, I'm not as childish as some,' he said. 'I'd help if I were able. But my mind is blank, I tell you. I haven't had an original thought in weeks. Call it fear of death paralyzing me. Call it a sort of impotence. I don't care what you call it. Because you don't care either. No one has offered me friendship, company, anything. I have been left alone in the dark and the cold. Do you wonder that my mind is frozen?'

Lindgren looked away, hiding what expressions chased across her. When she confronted Nilsson again, she had put on calm.

'I can't say how sorry I am, Elof,' she told him. 'You are partly to blame yourself. You acted so, well, self-sufficient, we assumed you didn't want to be bothered. The way Olga Sobieski, for instance, doesn't want to. That's why she moved in with me. When you joined Hussein Sadek – '

'He keeps the panel closed between our halves,' Nilsson shrilled. 'He never raises it. But the soundproofing is imperfect. I hear him and his girls in there.'

'Now we understand.' Lindgren smiled. 'To be quite honest, Elof, I've grown bored with my current existence.'

Nilsson made a strangled noise.

'I believe we have some personal business to discuss,' Lindgren said. 'Do . . . do you mind, Constable?'

'No,' said Reymont. 'Of course not.' He left the cabin.

CHAPTER 15

Leonora Christine stormed through the galactic nucleus in twenty thousand years. To those aboard, the time was measured in hours. They were hours of dread, while the hull shook and groaned from stress, and the outside view changed from total darkness to a fog made blinding and blazing by crowded star clusters. The chance of striking a sun was not negligible; hidden in a dust cloud, it could be in front of the ship in one perceived instant. (No one knew what would happen to the star. It might go nova. But certainly the vessel would be destroyed, too swiftly for her crew to know they were dead.) On the other hand, this was the region where inverse tau mounted to values that could merely be estimated, not established with precision, absolutely not comprehended.

She had a respite while she crossed the region of clear space at the center, like passing through the eye of a hurricane. Foxe-Jameson looked into the viewscope at thronged suns – red, white, and neutron dwarfs, two- and three-fold older than Sol or its neighbors; others, glimpsed, unlike any ever seen or suspected in the outer galaxy – and came near weeping. 'Too bloody awful! The answers to a million questions, right here, and not a single instrument I can use!'

His shipmates grinned. 'Where would you publish?' somebody asked. Renascent hope was often expressing itself in a kind of gallows humor.

But there was no joking when Boudreau called a conference with Telander and Reymont. That was soon after the ship had emerged from the nebulae on the far side of the nucleus and headed back through the spiral arm whence she came. The scene behind was of a dwindling fireball, ahead of a gathering darkness. Yet the reefs had been run, the journey to the Virgo galaxies would take only a few more months of human life, the program of research and development on planet-finding techniques had been announced with high optimism. A dance and slightly drunken brawl was held in commons to celebrate. Its laughter, stamping, lilt of Urho Latvala's accordion drifted faintly down to the bridge.

'I should perhaps have let you enjoy yourselves like everybody else,' Boudreau said. His skin was shockingly sallow against hair and beard. 'But Mohandas Chidambaran gave me the results of his calculations from the latest readings after we emerged from the core. He felt I was best qualified to gauge the practical consequences . . . as if any rulebook existed for intergalactic navigation! Now he sits alone in his cabin and meditates. Me, when I got over being stunned, I thought I should notify you immediately.'

Captain Telander's visage drew tight, readying for a new blow. 'What is the result?' he asked.

'What is the subject?' Reymont added.

'Matter density in space before us,' Boudreau said. 'Within this galaxy, between galaxies, between whole galactic clusters. Given our present tau, the frequency shift of the neutral hydrogen radio emission, the instruments already built by the astronomical team obtain unprecedented accuracy.'

'What have they learned, then?'

Boudreau braced himself. 'The gas concentration drops off slower than we supposed. With the tau we will probably have by the time we leave the Milky Way galaxy . . . twenty million light-years out, halfway to the Virgo group . . . as nearly as can be determined, we will still not dare turn off the force fields.'

Telander closed his eyes.

Reymont spoke jerkily: 'We've discussed that possibility in the past.' The scar stood livid on his brow. 'That even between two clusters, we won't be able to make our repair. It's part of the reason why Fedoroff and Pereira want to improve the life support systems. You act as if you had a different proposal.'

'The one we talked about not long ago, you and I,' Boudreau said to the captain.

Reymont waited.

Boudreau told him in a voice turned dispassionate: 'Astronomers learned centuries back, a cluster or family of galaxies like our local group is not the highest form in which stars are organized. These collections of one or two dozen galaxies do, in turn, tend to occur in larger associations. Superfamilies – '

Reymont made a rusty laugh. 'Call them clans,' he suggested.

'*Hein?* Why . . . all right. A clan is composed of several

families. Now the average distance between members of a family – individual galaxies within a cluster – is, oh, say a million light-years. The average distance between one family and the next is greater, as you would expect: on the order of fifty million light-years. Our plan was to leave this family and go to the nearest beyond, the Virgo group. Both belong to the same clan.'

'Instead, if we're to have any hope of stopping, we'll have to leave the entire clan.'

'Yes, I am afraid so.'

'How far to the next one?'

'I can't say. I didn't take journals along. They would be a bit obsolete by now, no?'

'Be careful,' Telander warned.

Boudreau gulped. 'I beg the captain's pardon. That was a rather dangerous joke.' He went back to lecturing tone: 'Chidambaran doesn't believe anyone was sure. The concentration of galactic clusters drops off sharply at a distance of about sixty million light-years from here. Beyond that, it is a long way to other rich regions. Chidambaran guessed at a hundred million light-years, or somewhat less. Else the hierarchical structure of the universe would have been easier for astronomers to identify than it was.

'Surely, between clans, space is so close to a perfect vacuum that we won't need protection.'

'Can we navigate there?' Reymont snapped.

Sweat glistened on Boudreau's countenance. 'You see the hazard,' he said. 'We will be bound into the unknown more deeply than we dreamed. Accurate sightings and placements will be unobtainable. We shall need such a tau – '

'A minute,' Reymont said. 'Let me outline the situation in my layman's language to make sure I understand you.' He paused, rubbing his chin with a sandpapery sound (under the distant music), frowning, until his thoughts were marshaled.

'We must get . . . not only into interfamily, but interclan space,' he said. 'We must do this in a moderate shipboard time. Therefore we must run tau down to a value of a billionth or less. Can we do it? Evidently, or you wouldn't talk as you've done. I imagine the method is to lay a course within this family that takes us through the nucleus of at least one other galaxy. And then likewise through the next family – be it the Virgo cluster or a different one determined by our new flight pattern – through as many individual galaxies as possible, always accelerating.

'Once the clan is well behind us, we should be able to make our repair. Afterward we'll need a similar period of deceleration. And because our tau will be so low, and space so utterly empty, we'll be unable to steer. Not enough material will be there for the jets to work on, nor enough navigational data to guide us. We'll have to hope that we pass through another clan.

'We should do that. Eventually. By sheer statistics. However, we may be out yonder a long while indeed.'

'Correct,' Telander said. 'You do understand.'

They had begun to sing upstairs.

> ' – *But me and my true love will never meet again*
> *On the bonnie, bonnie banks of Loch Lomond.*'

'Well,' Reymont said, 'there doesn't appear to be any virtue in caution. In fact, for us it's become a vice.'

'What do you mean?' Boudreau asked.

Reymont shrugged. 'We need more than the tau for crossing space to the next clan, a hundred million light-years or however far off it is. We need the tau for a hunt which will take us past any number of them, maybe through billions of light-years, until we find one we can enter. I trust you can plot a course within this first clan that will give us that kind of speed. Don't worry about possible collisions. We can't afford worries. Send us through the densest gas and dust you can find.'

'You . . . are taking this . . . rather coolly,' Telander said.

'What am I supposed to do? Burst into tears?'

'That is why I thought you should also hear the news first,' Boudreau said. 'You can break it to the others.'

Reymont considered both men for a moment that

131

stretched. 'I'm not the captain, you know,' he reminded them.

Telander's smile was a spasm. 'In certain respects, Constable, you are.'

Reymont went to the closest instrument panel. He stood before its goblin eyes with head bent and thumbs hooked in belt. 'Well,' he mumbled. 'If you really want me to take charge.'

'I think you had better.'

'Well, in that case. They're good people. Morale is upward bound again, now that they see some genuine accomplishment of their own. I think they'll be able to realize, not just intellectually, but emotionally, that there's no human difference between a million and a billion, or ten billion, light-years. The exile is the same.'

'The time involved, though – ' Telander said.

'Yes.' Reymont looked at them again. 'I don't know how much more of our life spans we can devote to this voyage. Not very much. The conditions are too unnatural. Some of us can adapt, but I've learned that others can't. So we absolutely have to push tau down as low as may be, no matter what the dangers. Not simply to make the trip itself short enough for us to endure. But for the psychological need to do our utmost.'

'How is that?'

'Don't you see? It's our way of fighting back at the universe. *Vogue la galère.* Go for broke. Full steam ahead and damn the torpedoes. I think, if I can put the matter to our people in those terms, they'll rally. For a while, anyhow.'

> '*The wee birdies sing and the wild flowers spring,*
> *And in sunshine the waters are sleeping –* '

CHAPTER 16

The course out of the Milky Way was not straight; it zigzagged a little, as much as several light-centuries, to pass through the densest accessible nebulae and dust banks. Nevertheless, the time aboard was counted in days until she was in the marches of the spiral arm, outward bound into a nearly starless night.

Johann Freiwald brought Emma Glassgold a piece of equipment he had made to her order. As had been proposed, she was joining forces with Norbert Williams to devise long-range life detectors. The machinist found her trotting about in her laboratory, hands busy, humming to herself. The apparatus and glassware were esoteric, the smells chemically pungent, the background that endless murmur and quiver which told how the ship plunged forward; and somehow she might have been a new bride making her man a birthday cake.

'Thank you.' She beamed as she accepted the article.

'You look happy,' Freiwald said. 'Why?'

'Why not?'

His arm swept in a violent gesture. 'Everything!'

'Well . . . a disappointment about the Virgo cluster, naturally. Still, Norbert and I – ' She broke off, blushing. 'We have a fascinating problem here, a real challenge, and he's already made a brilliant suggestion about it.' She cocked her head at Freiwald. 'I've never seen you in this black a mood. What's become of that cheerful Nietzcheanism of yours?'

'Today we leave the galaxy,' he said. 'Forever.'

'Why, you knew – '

'Yes. I also knew, know I must die sometime, and Jane too, which is worse. That does not make it easier.' The big blond man exclaimed suddenly, imploringly: 'Do you believe we will ever stop?'

'I can't say,' Glassgold answered. She stood on tiptoe to pat his shoulder. 'It was not easy to resign myself to the possibility. I did, though, through God's mercy. Now I can accept whatever comes to us, and feel how good most of it is. Surely you can do the same, Johann.'

'I try,' he said. 'It is so dark out there. I never thought that I, grown up, would again be afraid of the dark.'

The great whirlpool of suns contracted and paled astern. Another began slowly growing forward. In the viewscope it was a thing of delicate, intricate beauty, jeweled gossamer. Beyond it, around it, more appeared, tiny smudges and points of radiance. Despite the Einsteinian shrinkage of space at *Leonora Christine's* velocity, they showed monstrously remote and isolated.

That speed continued to mount, not as fast as in the regions left behind – here, the gas concentration was perhaps a hundred thousandth of that near Sol – but sufficiently to bring her to the next galaxy in some weeks of her own time. Accurate observations were not to be had without radical improvements in astronomical technology: a task into which Nilsson and his team cast themselves with the eagerness of escapers.

Testing a photoconverter unit, he personally made a discovery. A few stars existed out here. He didn't know whether random perturbations had sent them drifting from their parental galaxies, uncountable billions of years ago, or whether they had actually formed in these deeps, in unknown fashion. By a grotesquely improbable chance, the ship passed near enough to one that he identified it – a dim, ancient red dwarf – and could show that it must have planets, from the glimpse his apparatus got before the system was swallowed anew by distance.

It was an eerie thought, those icy shadowy worlds, manyfold older than Earth, perhaps one or two with life upon them, and never a star to lighten their nights. When he told Lindgren about it, she said not to pass the information any further.

Several days later, returning home from work, he opened

the door to their cabin and found her present. She didn't notice him. She was seated on the bed, facing away, her eyes on a picture of her family. The light was turned low, dusking her but falling so coldly on her hair that it looked white. She strummed her lute and sang . . . to herself? It was not the merriment of her beloved Bellman. The language, in fact, was Danish. After a moment, Nilsson recognized the lyrics, Jacobsen's *Songs of Gurre*, and Schönberg's melodies for them.

The call of King Valdemar's men, raised from their coffins to follow him on the spectral ride that he was condemned to lead, snarled forth.

> *'Be greeted, King, here by Gurre Lake!*
> *Across the island our hunt we take,*
> *From stringless bow let the arrow fly*
> *That we have aimed with a sightless eye.*
> *We chase and strike at the shadow hart,*
> *And dew like blood from the wound will start.*
> *Night raven swinging*
> *And darkly winging,*
> *And leafage foaming where hoofs are ringing,*
> *So shall we hunt ev'ry night, they say,*
> *Until that hunt on the Judgment Day.*
> *Holla, horse, and holla, hound,*
> *Stop awhile upon this ground!*
> *Here's the castle which erstwhile was.*
> *Feed your horses on thistledown;*
> *Man may eat of his own renown.'*

She started to go on with the next stanza, Valdemar's cry to his lost darling; but she faltered and went directly to his men's words as dawn breaks over them.

> *'The cock lifts up his head to crow,*
> *Has the day within him,*
> *And morning dew is running red*
> *With rust, from off our swords.*
> *Past is the moment!*
> *Graves are calling with open mouths,*

And earth sucks down ev'ry light-shy horror.
Sink ye, sink ye!
Strong and radiant, life comes forth
With deeds and hammering pulses.
And we are death folk,
Sorrow and death folk,
Anguish and death folk.
To graves! To graves! To dream-bewildered sleep –
Oh, could we but rest peaceful!'

For a little space there was silence. Nilsson said, 'That strikes too near home, my dear.'

She looked about. Weariness had laid a pallor on her face. 'I wouldn't sing it in public,' she answered.

Concerned, he went to her, sat down by her side and asked: 'Do you really think of us as being on the Wild Hunt of the damned? I never knew.'

'I try not to let on.' She stared straight before her. Her fingers plucked shivering chords from the lute. 'Sometimes – We are now at about the million-year mark, you know.'

He laid an arm around her waist. 'What can I do to help, Ingrid? Anything?'

She shook her head the least bit.

'I owe you so much,' he said. 'Your strength, your kindness, yourself. You made me back into a man.' With difficulty: 'Not the best man alive, I admit. Not handsome or charming or witty. I often forget even to try to be a good partner to you. But I do want to.'

'Of course, Elof.'

'If you, well, have grown tired of our arrangement . . . or simply want more, more variety – '

'No. None of that.' She put the lute aside. 'We have this ship to get to harbor, if ever we can. We dare not let anything else count.'

He gave her a stricken glance; but before he could inquire just what she meant, she smiled, kissed him, and said: 'Still, we could use a rest. A forgetting. You can do something for me, Elof. Draw our liquor ration. Help yourself to most of it; you're sweet when you've dissolved

your shyness. We'll invite somebody young and ungloomy --
Luis, I think, and Maria - and laugh and play games and
be foolish in this cabin and empty a pitcher of water over
anybody who says anything serious . . . . Will you do that?'
    'If I can,' he said.

Leonora Christine entered the next galaxy in its equatorial
plane, to maximize the distance she would traverse through
its wealth of gas and star dust. Already on the fringes,
where the suns were as yet widely scattered, she began to
bound at high acceleration. The fury of that passage
vibrated ever more strongly and noisily through her.
    Captain Telander kept the bridge. Seemingly he had
little control. The commitment was made; the spiral arm
curved ahead like a road shining blue and silver. Occasional
giant stars came sufficiently close to show in the now
modified screens, distorted with the speed effects that sent
them whirling past as if they were sparks blown by the
wind that shouted against the ship. Occasional dense
nebulae enclosed her in night or in the fluorescence of hot
newborn stellar fires.
    Lenkei and Barrios were the men who counted then,
conning her manually through that fantastic hundred-
thousand-year plunge. The displays before them, the
intercom voices of Navigator Boudreau explaining what
appeared to lie ahead or Engineer Fedoroff warning of
undue stresses, gave them some guidance. But the vessel
had gotten too swift, too massive for much veering; and
under these conditions, once-reliable instruments were
turned into Delphic oracles. Mostly the pilots flew on skill
and instinct, perhaps on prayer.
    Captain Telander sat throughout those shipboard hours,
so unmoving that you might have thought him dead. A few
times he bestirred himself. ('Heavy concentration of stuff
identified, sir. Could be too thick for us. Shall we try to
evade?') Responses came from him. ('No, carry on, take
every opportunity to bring down tau, if you estimate even
fifty-fifty odds in our favor.') Their tone was calm and
unhesitant.

The clouds around the nucleus were thicker and made heavier weather than those in the home galaxy. Thunders toned in the hull, which rocked and bucked to accelerations that changed faster than could be compensated. Equipment oroke from its containers and smashed; lights flickered, went but, were somehow rekindled by sweating, cursing men with flash beams; folk in darkened cabins awaited their deaths. 'Proceed on present course,' Telander ordered; and he was obeyed.

And the ship lived. She broke through into starry space and started out the other side of the immense Catherine wheel. In little more than an hour, she had re-entered intergalactic regions. Telander announced it without fanfare. A few people cheered.

Boudreau came before the captain, trembling with reaction but his features altogether alive. '*Mon Dieu*, sir, we did it! I was not sure it would be possible. I would not have had the courage, me, to issue the commands you did. You were right! You won us everything we hoped for!'

'Not yet,' said the seated man. His inflection was unchanged. He looked past Boudreau. 'Have you corrected your navigational data? Will we be able to use any other galaxies in this family?'

'Why . . . well, yes. Several, although some are small elliptical systems, and we will probably only manage to cut a corner across others. Too high a speed. By the same token, however, we should have less trouble and hazard each time, considering our mass. And we can certainly use at least two other galactic families, maybe three, in similar fashion.' Boudreau tugged his beard. 'I estimate we will be into, er, interclan space – well into it, so we can make those repairs – in another month.'

'Good,' Telander said.

Boudreau gave him a close regard and was shocked. Beneath its careful expressionlessness, the captain's countenance was that of a man drained empty.

Dark.

The absolute night.

Instruments, straining magnification and amplification, reconverting wave lengths, identified some glimmer in that pit. Human senses found nothing, nothing.

'We're dead.' Fedoroff's words echoed in earplugs and skulls.

'I feel alive,' Reymont replied.

'What else is death but the final cutting off? No sun, no stars, no sound, no weight, no shadow – ' Fedoroff's breath was ragged, too clear over a radio which no longer carried the surf noise of cosmic interference. His head was invisible against empty space. His suit lamp threw a dull puddle of light onto the hull that was reflected and lost in horrible distances.

'Let's keep moving,' Reymont urged.

'Who're you to give orders?' demanded another man. 'What do you know about Bussard engines? Why are you out with this work party anyhow?'

'I can manage myself in free fall and armor,' Reymont told him, 'and so provide you an extra pair of hands. I know we'd better get the job done fast. Which seems to be more than you bagelbrains realize.'

'What's the hurry?' Fedoroff mocked. 'We have eternity. We're dead, remember.'

'We will indeed be dead if we're caught, forceshields down, in anything like a real concentration of matter,' Reymont retorted. 'It'd take less than one atom per cubic meter to kill us with our present tau – which puts the next galactic clan only weeks away.'

'What of it?'

'Well, are you absolutely certain, Fedoroff, that we won't strike an embryo galaxy, family, clan . . . some enormous hydrogen cloud, still dark, still falling in on itself . . . at any instant?'

'At any millennium, you mean,' the chief engineer said. But, evidently stung out of his dauntedness, he started aft from the main personnel lock. His gang followed.

It was, in truth, a flitting of ghosts. No wonder he, never a coward, had briefly heard the wingbeats of the Furies. One had thought of space as black. But now one remember..

ed that it had been full of stars. Any shape had been silhouetted athwart suns, clusters, constellations, nebulae, sister galaxies; oh, the cosmos was pervaded with light! The *inner* cosmos. Here was worse than a dark background. Here was no background. None whatsoever. The squat, unhuman forms of spacesuited men, the long curve of the hull, were seen as gleams, disconnected and fugitive. With acceleration ended, weight was ended also. Not even the slight differential-gravity effects of being in orbit existed. A man moved as if in an infinite dream of swimming, flying, falling. And yet . . . he remembered that this weightless body of his bore the mass of a mountain. Was there a real heaviness in his floating; or had the constants of inertia subtly changed, out here where the metric of space-time was flattened to nearly a straight line; or was it an illusion, spawned in the tomb stillness which engulfed him? What was illusion? What was reality? Was reality?

Roped together, clinging with frantic bondsoles to the ship's metal (curious, the horror one felt of getting somehow pitched loose – extinction would be the same as if that had happened in the lost little spaceways of the Solar System – but the thought of blazing across gigayears as a stellar-scale meteor was peculiarly lonely), the engineer detail made their way along the hull, past the spidery framework of the hydromagnetic generators. Those ribs seemed terribly frail.

'Suppose we can't fix the decelerator half of the module,' came a voice. 'Do we go on? What happens to us? I mean, won't the laws be different on the edge of the universe? Won't we turn into something awful?'

'Space is isotropic,' Reymont barked into the blackness. ' "The edge of the universe" is gibberish. And let's start by supposing we can fix the stupid machine.'

He heard a few oaths and grinned like a carnivore. When they halted and began to secure their lifelines individually to the ion drive girders, Fedoroff laid his helmet against Reymont's for a private talk carried by conduction.

'Thanks, Constable,' he said.

'What for?'

'Being such a prosaic bastard.'

'Well, we have a prosaic job of repair to do. We may have come a long way, we may by now have outlived the race that produced us, but we haven't changed from a variety of proboscis monkey. Why take ourselves so mucking seriously?'

'Hm. I see why Lindgren insisted I let you come along.' Fedoroff cleared his throat. 'About her.'

'Yes.'

'I . . . I was angry . . . at your treatment of her. It was mainly that. Of course, I was, uh, humiliated personally. But a man should be able to get over that. I cared for her, though, very much.'

'Forget it,' Reymont said.

'I cannot do that. But maybe I can understand a little better than I let myself do in the past. You must have hurt too. And now, for her own reasons, she has gone from both of us. Shall we shake hands and be friends once more, Charles?'

'Surely. I've wanted this myself. Good men are hard to come by.' Gauntlets groped to find each other in the murk and clasp.

'All right.' Fedoroff switched his transmitter back on and pushed clear of the ship. 'Let's get aft and have a look at the problem.'

CHAPTER 17

Light began to glimmer ahead, a scattering of starlike points which waxed, in numbers and brightness, toward glory. Their dominion widened; presently the viewscope showed them occupying nearly half of heaven; and still that area grew and brightened.

They were not stars forming those strange constellations. They were, at first, entire families of galaxies making up a clan. Later, as the ship advanced, they broke into clusters and then into separate members.

The viewscope's reconstruction of this stationary-observer sight was only approximate. From the spectra received, a computer estimated what the Doppler shift, and thus the aberration, must be, and made corresponding adjustments. But these were nothing except estimates.

It was believed that the clan lay about three hundred million light-years from home. But no charts existed for these deeps, no standards of measurement. The probable error in the derived value of tau was huge. Factors like absorption simply were not in any reference work aboard.

Leonora Christine might have sought a less remote destination, for which more reliable data were tabulated. However – bearing in mind that at ultra-low tau she was not very steerable – that route would have taken her through less matter within the Milky Way-Andromeda-Virgo clan. She would have gained less speed; and now she was running so close to *c* that every increment made a significant difference. Paradoxically, shipboard time to the nearest possible target would have been more than to this one.

And it was not known, either, how long her people could endure.

The cheer brought by the repair of the decelerator was short-lived. For neither half of the Bussard module could work in interclan space. Here the primordial gas had finally gotten too thin. For weeks, therefore, the ship must go powerless on a trajectory set by the eldritch ballistics of relativity. Within her hull was weightlessness. There was some talk of using lateral ion jets to put a spin on her and thus provide centrifugal pseudo-gravity. Despite her size, it would have generated radial and Coriolis effects that were too troublesome. She had not been designed nor had her folk been trained for such.

They must bear the weeks, while the geological epochs passed by outside.

Reymont opened the door to his cabin. Weariness made him careless. Bracing himself a trifle too hard against the bulkhead, he let go the handhold and was propelled away. For a moment he cartwheeled in mid-air. Then he bumped into the opposite side of the corridor, pushed, and darted back across. Once within the cabin, he grabbled another bar before shutting the door behind him.

At this hour, he had expected Chi-Yuen Ai-Ling to be asleep. But she floated wakeful, a few centimeters off their joined beds, a single line anchoring her. As he entered, she switched off the library screen with a quickness that showed she hadn't really been paying attention to the book projected on it.

'Not you too?' Reymont's question seemed loud. They had been so long accustomed to the engine pulse as well as the force of acceleration that free fall still brimmed the ship with silence.

'What?' Her smile was tentative and troubled. They had had scant contact lately. He had too much work under these changed conditions, organizing, ordering, cajoling, arranging, planning. He would come here merely to snatch what slumber he might.

'Have you also become unable to rest in zero gee?' he asked.

'No. That is, I can. A strange, light sort of sleep, filled with dreams, but I seem fairly refreshed afterward.'

'Good,' he sighed. 'Two more cases have developed.'

'Insomniac, you mean?'

'Yes. Verging on nervous collapse. Every time they do drift off, you know, they wake again screaming. Nightmares. I'm not sure whether weightlessness alone does it to them, or if that's only the last thing needed for breaking stress. Neither is Urho Latvala. I was just conferring with him. He wanted my opinion on what to do, now that he's running short of psychodrugs.'

'What did you suggest?'

Reymont grimaced. 'I told him who I thought unconditionally had to have them, and who might survive awhile without.'

'The trouble isn't simply the psychological effect, you realize,' Chi-Yuen said. 'It is the fatigue. Pure physical tiredness, from trying to do things in a gravityless environment.

'Of course.' Reymont hooked one leg around the bar to hold himself in place and started to unfasten his coverall. 'Quite unnecessary. The regular spacemen know how to cope, and you and I and a few others. We don't get worn out trying to coordinate our muscles. It's those ground-lubber scientists who do.'

'How much longer, Charles?'

'Like this? Who knows? They plan to reactivate the force fields, at minimum strength off the interior power plant, tomorrow. A precaution, in case we strike denser material sooner than expected. The last estimate I heard for when we'll reach the fringes of the clan is a week.'

She relaxed in relief. 'We can stand that. And then ... we will be making for our new home.'

'Hope so,' Reymont grunted. He stored his clothes, shivered a little though the air was warm, and took out a pair of pajamas.

Chi-Yuen started. Her tether jerked her to a stop. 'What do you mean by that? Don't you know?'

'Look, Ai-Ling,' he said in an exhausted tone, 'you've been briefed like everybody else on our instrumentation problems. How in hell's flaming name can you expect an answer to anything?'

'I'm sorry – '

'Are the officers to blame if the passengers don't listen to their reports, won't understand?' Reymont's voice lifted in anger. 'Some of you are going to pieces again. Some of you have barricaded yourselves with apathy, or religion, or sex, or whatever, till nothing registers on your memories. Most of you – well, it *was* healthy to work on those R & D projects, but that's become a defense reaction in its own right. Another way of narrowing your attention till you exclude the big bad universe. And now, when free fall prevents you carrying on, you likewise crawl into your nice hidey-holes.' Lashingly: 'Go ahead. Do what you want. The whole wretched lot of you. Only don't come and peck at me any longer. D'you hear?'

He yanked the pajamas on, soared to the bed, and clipped

the safety line around his waist. Chi-Yuen moved to embrace him.

'Oh, love,' she whispered. 'I'm sorry. You are so tired, are you not?'

'Been hard on us all,' he said.

'Most on you.' Her fingers traced the cheekbones standing out under taut skin, the deep lines, the sunken and blood-shot eyes. 'Why don't you rest?'

'I'd like to.'

She maneuvred his mass into a stretched-out position and drew herself closer yet. Her hair floated across his face, smelling of sunshine on Earth. 'Do,' she said. 'You can. For you, isn't it good not to be heavy?'

'M-m-m . . . yes, in a way . . . . Ai-Ling, you know Iwasaki pretty well. Do you think he can manage without tranquilizers? The doctor and I weren't sure.'

'Hush.' Her palm covered his mouth. 'None of that.'

'But – '

'No, I will not have it. The ship isn't going to fall apart if you get one decent night's sleep.'

'Well . . . well . . . maybe not.'

'Close your eyes. Let me stroke your forehead – there. Isn't that better already? Now think of nice things.'

'Like what?'

'Have you forgotten? Think of home. No. Best not that, I suppose. Think of the home we are going to find. Blue sky. Warm bright sun, light falling through leaves, dappling the shade, blinking on a river; and the river flows, flows, flows, singing you to sleep.'

'Um-m-m.'

She kissed him very lightly. 'Our own house. A garden. Strange colorful flowers. Oh, but we will plant seeds from Earth too, roses, honeysuckle, apple, rosemary for remembrance. Our children . . . '

He stirred. The fret returned to him. 'Wait a minute, we can't make personal commitments. Not yet. You might not want, uh, any given man. I'm fond of you, of course, but – '

She brushed his lids shut again before he saw the pain on her. 'We are daydreaming, Charles,' she laughed low.

145

'Stop being all solemn and literal-minded. Just think about children, everyone's children, playing in a garden. Think about the river. Forests. Mountains. Bird song. Peace.'

He tightened an arm around her slenderness. 'You're a good person.'

'You are yourself. A good person who ought to be cuddled. Would you like me to sing you to sleep?'

'Yes.' His words were becoming indistinct. 'Please. I like Chinese music.'

She continued smoothing his brow while she drew breath.

The intercom circuit clicked shut. 'Constable,' said Telander's voice, 'are you there?'

Reymont snapped awake. 'Don't,' Chi-Yuen begged.

'Yes,' Reymont said, 'here I am.'

'Would you come to the bridge? Confidential.'

'Aye, aye.' Reymont undid his lifeline and pulled the pajama top over his head.

'They could not give you five minutes, could they?' Chi-Yuen said.

'Must be serious,' he answered. 'Don't mention it around until you hear from me.' In a few motions he had resumed coverall and shoes and was on his way.

Telander and, surprisingly, Nilsson awaited him. The captain looked as if he had been struck in the belly. The astronomer was excited but had not wholly lost his self-command of recent months. He clutched a bescribbled sheet of paper.

'Navigation difficulties, eh?' Reymont deduced. 'Where's Boudreau?'

'This doesn't concern him immediately,' Nilsson said. 'I have been computing the significance of observations I've made with the newest instruments. I have reached a, ah, frustrating conclusion.'

Reymont wrapped fingers around a grip and hung in the stillness, regarding them. The fluorolight cast the hollows of his face into shadow. The gray streaks which had lately appeared in his hair stood forth sharp by contrast. 'We can't make that galactic clan ahead of us after all,' he foretold.

'That's right.' Telander drooped.

'No, not right in a strict sense,' Nilsson declared fussily. 'We will pass through. In fact, we will pass through not only the general region, but – if we choose – through quite a fair number of galaxies within certain of the families which comprise the clan.'

'You can distinguish that much detail already?' Reymont wondered. 'Boudreau couldn't.'

'I told you I have new equipment, with its balkiness now tinkered out,' Nilsson said. 'You recollect that after Ingrid gave me some special lessons, I became able to work in free fall with a degree of efficiency. The precision of my data seems even more than hoped for when, ah, we instigated the project. Yes, I have a reasonably accurate map of that part of the clan which we might traverse. On such basis, I have calculated what options are open to us.'

'Get to the point, God damn you!' Reymont yelled. At once he curbed himself, inhaled, and said: 'Apologies. I'm a little overwrought. Please go on. Once we get in where the jets have a decent amount of matter to work on, why can't we brake?'

'We can,' Nilsson replied quickly. 'Certainly we can. But our inverse tau is immense. Remember, we acquired it by passing through the densest attainable portions of several galaxies, en route to interclan space. It was necessary. I don't dispute the wisdom of the decision. Nevertheless, the result is that we are limited in what paths we can take that intersect the space occupied by this clan. The paths form a rather narrow conoidal volume, as you might guess.'

Reymont gnawed his lip. 'And it turns out there doesn't happen to be enough matter in that cone.'

'Correct.' Nilsson's head bobbed. 'Among other things, the difference in velocity between us and these galaxies, due to the expansion of space, reduces the effectiveness of our Bussard engine more than it reduces the amount of deceleration required.'

His professional manner was returning to him: 'At best, we will emerge on the other side of the clan – after an estimated six months of ship's time under deceleration, mind you – with a tau that remains on the order of ten to the minus third or fourth power. No further important change of velocity can be made in the space beyond, interclan space. Hence it would be impossible for us to reach another clan – given that high a value of tau – before we die of old age.'

The pompous voice cut off, the beady eyes looked expectant. Reymont met them rather than Telander's sick, gutted stare. 'Why am I being told this, and not Lindgren?' he asked.

A tenderness made Nilsson, briefly, another man. 'She works cruelly hard. What can she do here? I thought I had best let her sleep.'

'Well, what can *I* do?'

'Give me . . . us . . . your advice,' Telander said.

'But sir, you're the captain!'

'We have been over this ground before, Carl. I can, well, yes, I suppose I can make the decisions, issue the commands, order the routines, which will take us crashing on through space.' Telander extended his hands. They trembled like autumn leaves. 'More than that I can no longer do, Carl. I have not the strength left. You must tell our shipmates.'

'Tell them we've failed?' Reymont grated. 'Tell them, in spite of everything we did, we're damned to fly on till we go crazy and die? You don't want much of me, do you, Captain?'

'The news may not be that bad,' Nilsson said.

Reymont snatched at him, missed, and hung with a raw noise in his throat. 'We have some hope?' he managed finally.

The fat man spoke with a briskness that turned his pedantry into a sort of bugle call:

'Perhaps. I have no worthwhile data. The distances are too vast. We cannot choose another specific galactic clan and aim for it. We would see it with too great an inaccuracy, and across too many millions of years of time. However, I do believe we can base a hope on the laws of chance.

'Someplace, eventually, we could meet the right configuration. Either an especially large clan through whose galaxy-densest portions we can lay a course; or else two or three clans, rather close to each other, more or less along a straight line, so that we can pass through them in succession; or else one whose velocity with respect to us happens to be favorable. Do you see? If we could come upon something like that, we would be in reasonable shape. We would be able to brake in a few years of ship's time.'

'What are the odds?' Reymont's words clanked.

Now Nilsson shook his head. 'I cannot say. Perhaps not too bad. This is a big and varied cosmos. If we continue sufficiently long, I should imagine we have a finite probability of encountering what we need.'

'How long is sufficiently long?' Reymont made a gesture to halt. 'Don't bother answering. I can tell. It's on the order of billions of years. Tens of billions, maybe. That means we've got to have a lower tau yet. A tau so low that we can actually circumnavigate the universe . . . in years or in months. And that, in turn, means we can't start slowing as we enter this clan up ahead. No. We accelerate again. After we've passed through – well, we should have a shorter period of ship's time in free fall than the current one has been, until we strike another clan. Probably there, too, we'll find it advisable to accelerate, running tau still lower. Yes, I know, that makes it still harder to find a place where we can come to rest; but anything else gives us no measurable chance at all, right?

'I expect we'll be taking every opportunity to accelerate that we come upon, till we see a journey's end we can make use of, if we ever do. Agreed?'

Telander shuddered. 'Can any of us hold to it?' he said.

'We must,' Reymont stated. Once more he spoke crisply. 'I'll figure out a tactful way to announce your news. It was among the possibilities that have been discussed by nearly everyone. That helps. I'll have the few men I can trust ready . . . no, not for violence. Ready with leadership, steadiness, encouragement. And we'll embark on a general training program for weightlessness. No reason why it has to cause trouble. We'll teach every last one of those ground-lubbers how to handle himself in zero gee. How to sleep. By

God, how to hope!' He smote his palms together with a pistol sound.

'Don't forget, we can depend on some of the women too,' Nilsson said.

'Yes. Certainly. Like Ingrid Lindgren.'

'Like her indeed.'

'M-hm. I'm afraid you will have to go rouse her, Elof. We've got to assemble our cadre – the unbreakables; the people who understand people – assemble them and plan this thing. Start suggesting names.'

CHAPTER 18

The reaches of space-time cannot be numbered by man's familiar integers. They cannot even be honestly counted by orders of magnitude. To feel this fact, recapitulate:

Leonora Christine spent most of a year getting within 1 per cent of light velocity. The time aboard was about the same, because the value of tau only began to drop sharply when she was quite near c. During that initial period, she covered half a light-year of space, approximately five trillion kilometers.

Thereafter the decrease became constantly more swift. Aided by the higher acceleration now possible, she required somewhat under two more years, in her own measure, to get about ten light-years from Earth. That was where she met her grief.

The decision being made to seek the Virgo cluster of galaxies, she must gain such a tau that she could bridge the distance in a tolerable shipboard time. At maximum acceleration – a maximum which increased as she traveled – she swung half around the Milky Way and into its heart in a little more than one year. According to the cosmos, it took better than a hundred millennia.

In the Sagittarian clouds, she won a tau which brought her out of her native galaxy in days. Then her people discovered that the vacuum between the family of star groups they were in and the Virgo assemblage at which their plans were aimed was not hard enough. They must go beyond the entire clan.

In intergalactic space, *Leonora Christine* remained able to pile on speed. It took her weeks to fare a couple of million light-years to a chosen neighbor galaxy. Spanning this in hours, she filled herself so full of kinetic energy that she crossed a similar distance in days . . . and presently she used a week or so to depart from her original cluster and reach another one . . . through which she passed quite rapidly . . . .

She coasted across the almost total emptiness of interclan space; meanwhile her engineers fixed the damaged unit. Although without acceleration, she needed only a pair of her own months to lay two or three hundred million light-years behind her.

The accessible mass of the whole galactic clan that was her goal proved inadequate to brake that velocity.

Therefore she did not try. Instead, she used what she swallowed to drive forward all the faster. She traversed the domain of this second clan – with no attempt at manual control, simply spearing through a number of its member galaxies – in two days.

On the far side, again into hollow space, she fell free. The stretch to the next attainable clan was on the order of another hundred million light-years. She made the passage in about a week.

When she arrived there, of course, she spent the star stuff she found to force herself still closer to the ultimate speed.

'No – don't – look out!'

Margarita Jimenes missed the handhold that would have checked her flight. Scrabbling for it, she struck the bulkhead, caromed, and floundered in air.

'*Ad i chawrti!*' Boris Fedoroff snorted.

He gauged vectors and launched himself to intercept her. It was not a conscious calculation; that would have been impossibly cumbersome. Like a hunter who aimed for a moving target, he used the skills and multiple senses of his body – angular diameters and shifts, muscle pressures and tensions, kinesthesia, the unseen but exactly known configuration of every joint, the several time derivatives of each of these factors and many more – his organism, a machine created with incomprehensible complexity and precision and, as it soared, beauty.

He had a ways to fly. They were on Number Two deck, well aft near the engine rooms. It was devoted to storage; but a major part of the materials it had held were now fashioned into objects. Where the cargo had been was a cavernous, echoing space, coldly lit, seldom visited. Fedoroff had brought his woman there for some private instruction in free-fall techniques. She was doing miserably in the classes that Lindgren had decreed for groundlubbers.

She spun before him, head lost among loose ringlets, arms and legs and breasts flopping. Sweat oiled her bare skin and broke off in globules that glittered around her like midges. 'Relax, I tell you,' Fedoroff called. 'The first damn thing you must learn is, "Relax".'

He passed within reach and grabbed her at the waist. Linked, the two of them formed a new system that spun on a crazy axis as it drifted toward the opposite bulkhead. Vestibular processes registered their outrage in giddiness and nausea. He knew how to suppress that reaction; and he had given her an antispacesickness pill before the lesson started.

Nevertheless she vomited.

He could do nothing except hold her through their trajectory. The first upheaval caught him by surprise and struck him in the face. Thereafter he clasped her back against belly. His free hand swatted at stinking yellow liquid and gobbets. Inhaled under these conditions, the stuff could choke a person.

When they hit metal, he snatched the nearest support, an empty rack. Hooking an elbow joint in it, he could use both arms to keep her and soothe her. Eventually the dry phase passed too.

'Are you better?' he asked.

She shivered and mumbled, 'I want to be clean.'

'Yes, yes, we'll find a bath. Wait here. Hang on, don't let go. I'll come in a few minutes.' Fedoroff shoved free again.

He must close the ventilators before the splashed foulness got drawn into the ship's general air system. Afterward he could see about catching it with a vacuum cleaner. He would do that himself. If he detailed another man to this mess, the fellow might do more than resent it. He might start a rumor about –

Fedoroff's teeth slammed together. He finished his precautions and dove back to Jimenes.

Though still white-faced, she appeared in command of her movements. 'I'm dreadfully sorry, Boris.' Her speech came hoarse out of a larynx burned by stomach acid. 'I should never have agreed . . . to come this far . . . from a suction toilet.'

He poised in front of her and asked grimly, 'How long have you been puking?'

She shrank away. He caught her before she drifted loose. His clasp was savage on her wrist. 'When was your last period?' he demanded.

'You saw – '

'I saw what could easily have been a fake. Especially considering how busy I've been in my work. Give me the truth!'

He shook her. Unanchored, her body was twisted at the shoulder. She screamed. He let her go as if she had turned incandescent. 'I didn't mean to hurt you,' he gasped. She bobbed from him. He got her just in time, hauled her back and held her tightly against his besmeared breast.

'Th-th-three months,' she stammered through her weeping.

He let her cry while he stroked the matted hair. When she was done, he helped her to a bathroom. They sponged each other fairly clean. The organic liquid they used had a pungency overriding the stench on them, but its volatilization was so rapid and thorough that Jimenes shuddered with chill. Fedoroff chucked the sponges into the chute of a laundry-bound conveyor and turned on a hot-air blower. He and she basked for minutes.

'Do you know,' he said after much silence, 'if we have solved the problem of hydroponics in zero gravity, we should be able to design something that will give us a real bath. Or even a shower.'

She didn't smile, only huddled near the grille. Her hair billowed backward.

Fedoroff stiffened. 'All right,' he said, 'how did it happen? Isn't the doctor supposed to keep track of every woman's contraceptive schedule?'

She nodded, not looking at him. Her reply was scarcely to be heard. 'Yes, One shot a year, though, for twenty-five of us . . . and he had, he has many things on his mind other than routine . . . '

'You didn't both forget?'

'No. I went to his office on my usual date. It's embarrassing when he has to remind a girl. He wasn't in. Out taking care of someone in trouble, maybe. His chart for us lay on his desk. I looked at it. Jane had been in for the same reason, I saw, this same day, probably an hour or two earlier. Suddenly I snatched his pen and wrote "OK" after my own name, in the space for this time. I scribbled it the way he does. It happened before I really knew what I was doing. I ran.'

'Why didn't you confess afterward? He's seen battier impulses than that since this ship went astray.'

'He should have remembered,' Jimenes said louder. 'If he decided that he must have forgotten I was in — why should I do his work for him?'

Fedoroff cursed and grabbed after her. He stopped his hand short of the bruised wrist. 'In the name of sanity!' he protested. 'Latvala's worked to death, trying to keep us functional. And you ask why you should help him?'

Her defiance grew more open. She faced him and said: 'You promised we could have children.'

'Why – well, yes, true, we want as many as we can, once we have a planet – '

'And if we do not find a planet? What then? Can't you improve the biosystems as you've been bragging?'

'We've put that aside in favor of the instrumentation project. It may take years.'

'A few babies won't make that much difference meanwhile . . . to the ship, the damned ship . . but the difference to *us* – '

He moved toward her. Her eyes widened. She crawled from him, handhold to handhold. 'No!' she yelled. 'I know what you're after! You'll never take my baby! He's yours too! If you . . . you cut my baby out of me – I'll kill you! I'll kill everyone aboard!'

'Quiet!' he bellowed. He backed off a little. She clung where she was, sobbing and baring teeth. 'I won't do a thing myself,' he said. 'We'll see the constable.' He went to the exit. 'Stay here. Pull yourself together. Think how you want to argue. I'll fetch clothes for us.'

On his errand, the sole words he uttered were through the intercom, requesting a private talk with Reymont. Nor did he speak to Jimenes, or she to him, on their way to their cabin.

When they were inside, she seized his arms. 'Boris, your own child, you can't – and Easter coming – '

He tethered her. 'Calm down,' he warned. 'Here.' He gave her a squeeze bottle with some tequila in it. 'This may help. Don't drink much. You'll need your wits about you.'

The door chimed. Fedoroff admitted Reymont and closed it again. 'Would you like a dram, Charles?' the engineer asked.

The features he confronted might have been a vizor on a war helmet. 'We'd better discuss your problem first,' said the constable.

'Margarita is pregnant,' Fedoroff told him.

Reymont floated quiet, lightly gripping a bar. 'Please – ' Jimenes began.

Reymont waved her to silence. 'How did that happen?' he inquired, softly as the ship's breath from the ventilators.

She tried to explain, and couldn't. Fedoroff put in in a few words.

'I see.' Reymont nodded. 'About seven months to go, hm? Why do you consult me? You should have gone directly to the first officer. She'll be the one in any event who disposes of the case. I have no power except to arrest you for a grave breach of regulations.'

'You – We are friends, I thought, Charles,' Fedoroff said.

'My duty is to the whole ship,' Reymont answered in the same monotone as before. 'I can't go along with anyone's selfish action that threatens the lives of the rest.'

'One tiny baby?' Jimenes cried.

'And how many more desired by others?'

'Must we wait forever?'

'It would seem proper to wait till you know what our future is likely to be. A child born here could have a short life and a grisly death.'

Jimenes locked fingers over her abdomen. 'You won't murder him! You won't!'

'Be still,' spat from Reymont. She choked but obeyed. He turned his gaze on Fedoroff. 'What are your views, Boris?'

Slowly, the Russian retreated until he was beside his woman. He drew her to him and said: 'Abortion is murder. This should not have happened, maybe, but I cannot believe my shipmates are murderers. I will die before I permit it.'

'We'd be in bad shape without you.'

'Exactly.'

'Well – ' Reymont averted his eyes. 'You haven't yet told me what you imagine I can do,' he said.

'I know what you can,' Fedoroff answered. 'Ingrid will want to save this life. She may not be able without your advice and backing.'

'Hm. Hm. So.' Reymont drummed the bulkhead. 'It isn't the worst thing for us, this,' he said at length, thoughtfully. 'There might even be some gains to make. If we can pass it off as an accident, an oversight, whatever, instead of a deliberate infraction . . . . It was, at that, in a way. Margarita acted insanely; still, how sane are any of us by now? . . . Hm. Suppose we announce a consequent relaxation of the rules. A very limited number of births will be authorized. We'll compute how many the ecosystem can stand and let the women who want draw lots. I doubt that many will . . . under present circumstances. The rivalry shouldn't be great. Having infants to coo over and help take care of, that might well relieve certain tensions.'

Briefly, his voice rose. 'Also, by God, they're a pledge of confidence. And a fresh reason to survive. Yes!'

Jimenes tried to reach him and embrace him. He warded her off. Above her weeping and laughter, he ordered the engineer: 'Get her calmed. I'll discuss this with the first officer. In due course, we'll all confer together. Meanwhile, no word or sign to anybody.'

'You . . . take the affair . . . coolly,' Fedoroff said.

'How else?' Reymont's answer was edged. 'Been too bloody much emotion around.' For another instant, the vizor lifted. This time a death's head looked out. 'Too bloody clawing much!' he shouted. He flung the door wide and whipped into the corridor.

Boudreau peered through the viewscope. The galaxy toward which *Leonora Christine* rushed showed as a blue-white haze on a darkling visual field. When he had finished, a scowl bent his brow. He walked to the main console. His footfalls thudded in the restored weight of an intrafamilial passage.

'It is not right,' he said. 'I have seen plenty of them; I know.' ·

'Do you mean the color?' Foxe-Jameson asked. The navigator had bidden the astrophysicist come to the bridge. 'Frequency seem too low for our speed? That's mainly due to simple space expansion, Auguste. The Hubble constant. We're overhauling galactic groups whose velocity gets higher and higher with respect to our starting point, the farther we travel. Good thing too. Otherwise the Doppler effect might present us with more gamma radiation than our material shielding can handle. And, to be sure, as you very well know, we're counting heavily on the same space expansion to help us into a situation where we can stop. Eventually the velocity changes in themselves ought to overbalance their reduction of Bussard efficiency.'

'That part is plain.' Boudreau leaned on the desk, shoulders hunched, brooding over the notes he had made. 'I tell you, however, I have watched each single galaxy we passed through, or in observation distance of, these months. I have grown familiar with their types. And gradually those types are changing.' He jerked his head at the viewscope. 'That up ahead, for instance, it is of the irregular sort, like the Magellanic Clouds at home – '

'I daresay, in these parts, the Magellanic Clouds count as home,' Foxe-Jameson murmured.

Boudreau chose to ignore the aside. 'It should have a high proportion of Population II stars,' he went on. 'From here we should be able to see many individual blue giants. Instead, we see none.

'All the spectra I take, to the extent I can interpret them, they are becoming different from what is normal for the types. No kind of galaxy looks right any more.'

He raised his eyes. 'Malcolm, what is happening?'

Foxe-Jameson appeared surprised. 'Why'd you pick me to query?' he countered.

'I had only a vague impression at first,' Boudreau said. 'I am not a real astronomer. Besides, I could not get accurate navigational sights. To obtain a value of tau, for instance, requires such a cat's cradle of assumptions that – *Bien*, when I finally felt sure the nature of space was altering, I approached Charles Reymont. You know how he puts down panic-mongers, and he is correct in that. He told me to call in one of your team, quietly, and report the answer back to him.'

Foxe-Jameson chortled. 'Why, you two pathetic beggars! Haven't you anything else to stew about? Actually, I thought it'd be common knowledge. So common that none of us pros happened to mention it, starved though everyone is for fresh conversation. Makes a chap wonder what else he's overlooking, eh?'

'*Qu'est-ce que c'est?*'

'Consider,' Foxe-Jameson said. He settled one thigh and

buttock on the desk. 'Stars evolve. They build heavier elements than hydrogen in thermonuclear reactions. If one is so big that it explodes, a supernova, at the end of its life, it scatters some of those atoms back into the interstellar medium. A more important process, though, if less spectacular, is the shedding of mass by smaller stars, the majority, in their red-giant stage on the way to extinction. New generations of stars and planets condense out of this enriched medium and add to it in their turn. Over the ages you get a rising proportion of metal-rich suns. That affects the over-all spectrum. But of course no star gives back more than a percentage of the material which formed it. Most matter stays locked in dense bodies, cooling toward absolute zero. So the interstellar medium becomes depleted. Space within the galaxies grows more clear. The rate of star formation declines.'

He gestured bow-ward. 'Finally you reach a point where little or no further condensation is possible. The energetic, short-lived blue giants burn themselves out and have no successors. The galaxy's luminous members are entirely dwarfs – at last nothing except cool, red, miserly Type Ms. Those are good for almost a hundred gigayears.

'I'd judge this galaxy we're aimed for isn't that far along yet. But it's getting there. It's getting there.'

Boudreau pondered. 'Then we won't gain as much speed per galaxy as we did before,' he said. 'Not if the interstellar gas and dust are being used up.'

'True,' Foxe-Jameson said. 'Don't fret. I'm sure ample will remain for our purposes. Every bit doesn't get collected in stars. Besides, we have the intergalactic medium, the intercluster, the interfamilial – thin, that, but usable at our present tau – and eventually we should be getting work out of the interclan gas itself.'

He clapped the navigator's back in friendly wise. 'We've come about three hundred megaparsecs now, remember,' he said. 'Which means about a thousand million years of time. You've got to expect some changes.'

Boudreau was less accustomed to astronomical concepts. 'You mean,' he whispered, 'the whole universe is growing enough older for us to notice?' It was the first time since his early youth that he had crossed himself.

The door to the interview room was shut. Chi-Yuen hesitated before pressing the chime button. When Lindgren let her in, she said timidly. 'They told me you were here alone.'

'Writing.' The first officer stood somewhat slumped; nonetheless she topped the planetologist by a head. 'A private place.'

'I hate to disturb you.'

'What I'm for, Ai-Ling. Sit down.' Lindgren went back behind her desk, which was covered with scrawled-on papers. The cabin hummed and trembled to irregular acceleration. More than a day of weight remained. *Leonora Christine* was bound through a clan of unprecedented size and opulence.

For a while, hope had lived that this might be the one where the ship could reach a halt within some member galaxy. Closer observation showed otherwise. Inverse tau had gotten too immense.

A faction had argued at general assembly that there ought to be limited deceleration anyhow, in order that requirements for stopping inside the next clan be less rigorous. One could not prove the contention wrong; not that much cosmography was known. One could only use statistics, as Nilsson and Chidambaran did, to prove that the *likelihood* of finding a resting place *seemed* greater if acceleration continued. The theorem was too involved for most persons to follow. The ship's officers elected to take it on faith and maintain full forward thrust. Reymont had had to quell some individuals whose objections approached mutiny.

Chi-Yuen perched herself on the edge of a visitors' chair. She was small and neat in high-collared red tunic, broad white slacks, hair brushed back with unwonted severity and held by an ivory comb. Lindgren contrasted in more than size. Her shirt was open at the neck, rolled up at the sleeves, smudged here and there; her hair was tousled, her eyes haunted.

'What are you writing, if I may ask?' Chi-Yuen ventured.
'A sermon,' Lindgren said. 'Not easy. I'm no writer.'
'You, a sermon?'

The left corner of Lindgren's mouth twitched slightly upward. 'Actually the captain's address at our Midsummer Day festivities. He can still conduct divine service, after a fashion. But for this he requested me to, ah, inspirit the troops in his name.'

'He is not a well man, is he?' Chi-Yuen inquired low.

The humor flickered out in Lindgren. 'No. I assume I can trust you not to blab that around. Even if everybody does suspect it.' She rested elbow on desk, forehead on hand. 'His responsibility is destroying him.'

'How can he blame himself? What choice has he except to let the robots move us onwards?'

'He cares.' Lindgren sighed. 'Also, this latest dispute. In his condition, that was more than he could take. He's not nervously prostrated, understand. Not quite. But he's no longer able to buck people.'

'Are we wise to hold a ceremony?' Chi-Yuen wondered.

'I don't know,' Lindgren said in a worn-out voice. 'I simply don't. Now when – we aren't announcing it, but we can't prevent computation and talk – when we're somewhere around the five- or six-billion-year mark. . . . ' Her head lifted, her hand fell. 'To celebrate something as purely Earth as Midsummer Day, *now when we have to start thinking of Earth as gone* – '

She seized both arms of her chair. For a moment the blue eyes were wild and blind. Then the straining body eased, muscle by muscle; she leaned into the seat until its swivel joint tilted with a creak; she said flatly: 'The constable persuaded me to go ahead with our rituals. Defiance. Reunification, after the past quarrel. Rededication, especially to that unborn baby. New Earth: We'll snatch it from God's grip yet. If God means anything, even emotionally, any more. Maybe I should lay off religion altogether. Carl didn't give me any details. Only the general idea. I'm supposed to be its best spokesman. Me. That tells you a good deal about our condition, doesn't it?'

She blinked, returning to herself. 'Apologies,' she said. 'I oughtn't to have dropped my problems on you.'

'They are everyone's problems, First Officer,' Chi-Yuen replied.

'Please. My name is Ingrid. Thanks, though. If I haven't told you before, let me say now, in your quiet way you're one of the key people aboard. A garden of calm — Well.' Lindgren bridged her fingers. 'What can I do for you?'

Chi-Yuen's glance fluttered to the desk. 'It's about Charles.'

The ends of Lindgren's nails whitened.

'He needs help,' Chi-Yuen said.

'He has his deputies,' Lindgren answered tonelessly.

'Who keeps them going except him? Who keeps us all going? You too, Ingrid. You depend on him.'

'Certainly.' Lindgren intertwined her fingers and strained them. 'You must realize — perhaps he never mentioned it to you in words, any more than to me or I to him; but it's obvious — there's no quarrel left between him and me. We eroded that away, working together. I wish him everything good.'

'Can you give him some of it, then?'

Lindgren's gaze sharpened. 'What do you mean?'

'He is tired. More tired than you imagine, Ingrid. And more alone.'

'His nature.'

'Maybe. Still, that was never any of the inhuman things he's had to be: a fire, a whip, a weapon, an engine. I've come to know him a little. I've watched him lately, how he sleeps, what few times he can. His defenses are used up. I hear him talk sometimes, in his dreams, when they aren't simply nightmares.'

Lindgren closed her hands on emptiness. 'What can we do for him?'

'Give him back a part of his strength. You can.' Chi-Yuen raised her eyes. 'You see, he loves you.'

Lindgren got up, paced the narrow stretch behind her desk, struck fist into palm. 'I've assumed obligations,' she said. The words wrenched her gullet.

'I know – '

'Not to smash a man, especially one we need. And not to . . . be promiscuous again. I have to be an officer, in everything I do. So does Carl.' Raw-voiced: 'He'd refuse!'

Chi-Yuen rose likewise. 'Can you spare this night?' she asked.

'What? What? No. Impossible, I tell you. Oh, I've the time, but impossible all the same. You'd better go.'

'Come with me.' Chi-Yuen took Lindgren by the hand. 'What scandal can there be if you visit the two of us in our cabin?'

The big woman stumbled after her. They went up the thrumming stairs to crew level. Chi-Yuen opened her door, led Lindgren through, closed it again. They stood alone amidst the ornaments and souvenirs of a country that died gigayears before, and regarded each other. Lindgren breathed in deep, quick draughts. Red pursued white across her face, down throat and bosom.

'He should be back soon,' Chi-Yuen said. 'He doesn't know. It is my gift to him. One night, at least: to tell him and show him how you never stopped feeling.'

She had separated the beds. Now she lowered the dividing partition. She did not quite forestall her tears.

Lindgren held her close for a moment, kissed her, and finished sealing her off. Then Lindgren waited.

CHAPTER 19

'Please,' Jane Sadler had implored. 'Come help him.'

'You can't?' Reymont asked.

She shook her head. 'I've tried. And I think I make matters worse. In his present condition. I being a woman.' She flushed. 'You savvy?'

'Well, I'm no psychologist,' Reymont said. 'However, I'll see what I can do.'

He left the bower where she had caught him at rest. The dwarfed trees, tumbling vines, moss, and blossoms made it a place of healing for him. But he noticed that comparatively few others went into these rooms any longer. Did such things remind them of too much?

Certainly no plans were being made for celebration of the autumnal equinox which impended on the ship's calendar – or any other holidays, for that matter. The Midsummer festival had been dishearteningly hushed.

In the gymnasium, a zero-gee handball game bounced from corner to corner. They were spacemen who played, though, and doggedly rather than gleefully. Most of the passengers came here for little except their compulsory exercises. They weren't showing great interest in meals, either: not that Carducci was doing an inspired job nowadays. One or two passersby gave Reymont a listless hail.

Farther down the corridor, a door stood open on a hobby shop. A lathe hummed, a cutting torch glowed blue, in the hands of Kato M'Botu and Yeshu ben-Zvi. Apparently they were making something for the recently resumed Fedoroff-Pereira ecological project, and had been crowded out of the regular facilities on the lower decks.

That was good as far as it went, but it didn't go any real distance. You had to be sure precisely what you were doing before you overhauled the systems on which life rested. As yet, and doubtless for years to come, matters were at the research stage. The undertaking could only engage the full attention of a few specialists, until actual construction began.

Nilsson's instrumental improvements had been an excellent work maker. Now that was drawing to a close, unless the astronomers could think up new inventions. Most of the labor was finished; cargo had been shifted, Number Two deck converted to an electronic observatory, its haywire tangle trimmed. The experts might tinker and refine, as well as lose themselves in their prodigious studies of the outer universe. For the bulk of the team, no task was left.

Nothing was left save to abide.

At each crisis, the folk had rallied. Yet each upsurge of hope peaked lower than the last, each withdrawal to misery went deeper. You would offhand have expected more reaction to the changed ruling on children, for instance. Exactly two women had applied for motherhood, and their last shots wouldn't wear off for months. The rest were interested, no doubt, in a fashion –

The ship quivered. Weight grabbed at Reymont. He barely avoided falling to the deck. A metal noise toned through the hull, like a basso profundo gong. It was soon over. Free flight resumed. *Leonora Christine* had gone through another galaxy.

Those passages were becoming more frequent by the day. Would she never meet the right configuration to stop? Ought she to start deceleration, if only to be doing something different?

Could Nilsson, Chidambaran, and Foxe-Jameson have miscalculated? Were they beginning to realize it? Was that why they'd worked late hours in the observatory, these past few weeks, and been so worried-looking and taciturn when they came out for food or sleep?

Well, no doubt Lindgren would get the information from Nilsson when it was confirmed, whatever it was.

Reymont floated along the stairwell to the crew deck. After a pause at his own cabin, he found the door he wanted, and chimed. Getting no response, he tried it. Locked. Sadler's adjoining door wasn't. He entered her side. The partition was down between her and her man. Reymont swung it out of the way.

Johann Freiwald floated at the end of his bedline. The husky shape was curled into an imitation of a fetus. But the eyes held awareness.

Reymont grasped a handhold, encountered that stare, and said noncommittally, 'I wondered why you haven't been around. Then I heard you aren't feeling well. Anything I can do for you?'

Freiwald grunted.

'You can do considerable for me,' Reymont went on. 'I need you pretty badly. You've been the best deputy – policeman, counselor, work-party boss, idea man – I've had through this whole thing. You can't be spared.'

Freiwald spoke with an effort. 'I shall have to be spared.'

'Why? What's the matter?'

'I can't go on any more. It's that simple. I can't.'

'Why not?' Reymont persisted. 'What jobs we have aren't hard, physically. Anyhow, you're tough. Weightlessness never bothered you. You're a machine-era boy, a practical chap, a lusty, earthy soul. Not one of those self-appointed delicates who have to be coddled every minute because their tender spirits can't *bear* a long voyage.' He sneered. 'Or are you one?'

Freiwald stirred. His unshaven cheeks darkened a trifle. 'I am a man,' he said. 'Not a robot. Eventually I start thinking.'

'My friend, do you imagine we would have survived this far if the officers, at any rate, did not spend every waking hour thinking?'

'I don't mean your damned measurements, computations, course adjustments, equipment modifications. That's from nothing but the instinct to stay alive. A lobster trying to climb out of a kettle has as much dignity. I ask myself, why? What are we really doing? What does it mean?'

'*Et tu, Brute*,' Reymont muttered.

Freiwald twisted about until his gaze was straight into the constable's. 'Because you are so callous. . . . Do you know what year this is?'

'No. Neither do you. The data are too uncertain. And if you wonder what the year would be at Sol, that's meaningless.'

'Be quiet! I know the whole simultaneity quacking. We have come something like fifty billion light-years. We are rounding the whole curve of space. If we returned this instant to the Solar System, we would not find anything. Our sun died long ago. It swelled and brightened till Earth was devoured; it became a variable, guttering like a candle

166

in the wind; it sank away to a white dwarf, an ember, an ash. And the other stars followed. Nothing can be left in our galaxy but waning red dwarfs, if that. Otherwise clinkers. The Milky Way has gone out. Everything we knew, everything that made us, is dead. Starting with the human race.'

'Not necessarily.'

'Then it's become something we could not comprehend. We are ghosts.' Freiwald's lips trembled. 'We hunt on and on, monomaniacs – ' Again acceleration thundered through the ship. 'There. You heard.' His eyes were white-rimmed, as if with fear. 'We passed through another galaxy. Another hundred thousand years. To us, part of a second.'

'Oh, not quite,' Reymont said. 'Our tau can't be that far down, can it? We probably quartered a spiral arm.'

'Destroying how many worlds? I know the figures. We are not as massive as a star. But our energy – I think we could pierce the heart of a sun and not notice.'

'Perhaps.'

'That's one section of our hell. That we've become a menace to – to – '

'Don't say it.' Reymont spoke earnestly. 'Don't think it. Because it isn't true. We're interacting with dust and gas, nothing else. We do transit many galaxies. They lie comparatively close together in terms of their own size. Within a cluster, the members are about ten diameters apart, often less. Single stars within a galaxy – that's another situation altogether. Their diameters are such a microscopic fraction of a light-year. In a nuclear region, the most crowded part . . . well, the separation of two stars is still like the separation of two men, one at either end of a continent. A big continent. Like Asia.'

Freiwald looked away. 'There is no more Asia,' he said. 'No more anything.'

'There's us,' Reymont answered. 'We're alive, we're real, we have hope. What else do you want? Some grandiose philosophical significance? Forget it. That's luxury. Our descendants will invent it, along with tedious epics about our heroism. We have the sweat, tears, blood' – his grin flashed – 'in short, the unglamorous bodily excretions. And what's bad about that? Your trouble is, you think a combination of acrophobia, sensory deprivation, and nervous strain is a metaphysical crisis. Myself, I don't despise our lobsterish instinct to survive. I'm glad we have one.'

Freiwald floated motionless.

Reymont crossed to him and squeezed his shoulder. 'I'm not belittling your difficulties,' he said. 'It *is* hard to keep going. Our worst enemy is despair; and it wrestles every one of us to the deck, every now and then.'

'Not you,' Freiwald said.

'Oh yes,' Reymont told him. 'Me too. I get my feet back, though. So will you. If you'll only stop feeling worthless because of a disability that is a perfectly normal temporary result of psychic exhaustion – as Jane understands better than you, young fellow – why, the disability will soon go away of itself. Afterward you'll see the rest of your problems in perspective and start coping once more.'

'Well –' Freiwald, who had tensed while Reymont spoke, relaxed the barest bit. 'Maybe.'

'I know. Ask the doctor if you don't believe me. If you want, I'll have him issue you some psychodrugs to hasten your recovery. My reason is that I do need you, Johann.'

The muscles beneath Reymont's palm softened further. He smiled. 'However,' he continued, 'I've got with me the only psychodrug I expect is called for.'

'What?' Freiwald looked 'up.'

Reymont reached under his tunic and extracted a squeeze bottle with twin drinking tubes. 'Here,' he said. 'Rank has its prvileges. Scotch. The genuine article, not that witch's brew the Scandinavians think is an imitation. I prescribe a hefty dose for you, and for myself too. I'd enjoy a leisurely talk. Haven't had any for longer than I can remember.'

They had been at it an hour, and life was coming back in Freiwald's manner, when the intercom said with Ingrid Lindgren's voice: 'Is the constable there?'

'Uh, yes,' Freiwald replied.

'Sadler told me,' the first officer explained. 'Could you come to the bridge, Carl?'

'Urgent?' Reymont asked.

'N-n-not really, I guess. The latest observations seem to indicate . . . further evolutionary changes in space. We may have to modify our cruising plan. I thought you might like to discuss it.'

'All right.' Reymont shrugged at Freiwald. 'Sorry.'

'Me also.' The other man considered the flask, shook his head sadly, and offered it back.

'No, you may as well finish it,' Reymont said. 'Not alone. Bad, drinking alone. I'll tell Jane.'

'Well, now.' Freiwald genuinely laughed. 'That's kind of you.'

Emerging, closing the door behind him, Reymont glanced the length of the corridor. No one else was in sight. He sagged, then, eyes covered, body shaking. After a minute he filled his lungs and started for the bridge.

Norbert Williams happened to come the other way along the stairs. 'Hi,' the chemist greeted.

'You're looking cheerier than most,' Reymont remarked.

'Yeah, I guess I am. Emma and I, we got talking, and we may have hit on a new gimmick to check at a distance whether a planet has our type of life. A plankton-type population, you see, ought to impart certain thermal radiation characteristics to ocean surfaces; and given Doppler effect, making those frequencies something we can properly analyze – '

'Good. Do work on it. And if you should co-opt others, I'll be glad.'

'Sure, we thought of that.'

'And would you pass the word that wherever she is, Jane Sadler's dismissed from work for the day? Her boy friend has something to take up with her.'

Williams' guffaw followed Reymont through the stair-well.

But the command deck was empty and still; and in the bridge, Lindgren stood watch alone. Her hands strained around the grips at the base of the viewscope. When she turned about at his entry, he saw that her face was quite without color.

He closed the door. 'What's wrong?' he said hushedly. 'You didn't let on?'

'No, of course not, when the business had to be fierce. What is it?'

She tried to speak and could not.

'Are more people due at this meeting?' Reymont asked.

She shook her head. He went to her, anchored himself with a leg wrapped around a rail and the other foot braced to the deck, and received her in his arms. She held him as tightly as she had done on their single stolen night.

'No,' she said against his breast. 'Elof and . . . Auguste Boudreau . . . they told me. Otherwise, just Malcolm and Mohandas know. They asked me to tell . . . the Old Man. They don't dare. Don't know how. I don't either. How to tell anyone.' Her nails bit through his tunic. 'Carl, what shall we do?'

He ruffled her hair awhile, staring across her head, feeling her heartbeat quick and irregular. Again the ship boomed and leaped; and soon again. The notes that rang through her were noticeably higher pitched than before. The draft from a ventilator blew cold. The metal around seemed to shrink inward.

'Go on,' he said at last. 'Tell me, *älskling*.'

'The universe – the whole universe – it's dying.'

He made a noise in his throat. Otherwise he waited.

At length she was able to pull far enough back from him that they could look into each other's eyes. She related in a slurred, hurried voice:

'We've come farther than we knew. In space and time. More than a hundred billion years. The astronomers began suspecting it when – I don't know. I only know what they've told me. Everybody's heard how the galaxies we see are getting dimmer. Old stars fading, new ones not being born. We didn't think it would affect us. All we were after was one little sun not too different from Sol. There ought to be many left. The galaxies have long lives. But now –

'The men weren't sure. The observations are hard to

make. But they started to wonder . . . if we might not have under-estimated the distance we've gone. They checked Doppler shifts extra carefully. Especially of late, when we seem to pass through more and more galaxies and the gas between them seems to be growing denser.

'They found that what they observed could not be explained in full by any tau we can possibly have. Another factor had to be involved. The galaxies are crowding together. The gas is being compressed. Space isn't expanding any longer. It's reached its limit and is collapsing inward again. Elof says the collapse will go on. And on. To the end.'

'We?' he asked.

'Who can tell? Except the figures show we can't stop. We could, I mean. But by the time we did, nothing would be left . . . except blackness, burned-out suns, absolute zero, death, death. Nothing.'

'We don't want that,' he said stupidly.

'No. What do we want?' Strange that she was not crying. 'I think – Carl, shouldn't we say good night? All of us, to each other? A last festival, with wine and candlelight. And afterward go to our cabins. You and I to ours. And love, if we can, and say good night. We have morphine for everyone. And oh, Carl, we're so tired. It will be so good to sleep.'

Reymont drew her close to him again.

'Did you ever read *Moby Dick*?' she whispered. 'That's us. We've pursued the White Whale. To the end of time. And now . . . that question. *What is man, that he should outlive his God?*'

Reymont put her from him, gently, and sought the viewscope. Looking forth, he saw, for a moment, a galaxy pass. It must be only some ten thousands of parsecs distant, for he saw it across the dark very large and clear. The form was chaotic. Whatever structure it had once had was disintegrated. It was a dull, vague redness, deepening at the fringes to the hue of clotted blood.

It drifted from his sight. The ship went through another, storm-shaken by it, but of that one nothing was visible.

Reymont hauled himself back to the command deck. Teeth gleamed in his visage. 'No!' he said.

CHAPTER 20

From the stage, he and she looked upon their assembled shipmates.

The gathering was seated, safety-harnessed into chairs whose legs were secured with bond grips to the gymnasium deck. Anything else would have been dangerous. Not that weightlessness prevailed. The past week had seen conditions change so rapidly that those who knew could not have deferred an explanation longer had they wanted to.

Between the tau which interstellar atoms now had with respect to *Leonora Christine*; and the compression of lengths in her own measurement because of that tau; and the dwindling radius of the cosmos itself: Her ramjets drove her at a goodly fraction of one gee across the outermost abysses of interclan space. And oftener and oftener came spurts of higher acceleration as she passed through galaxies. They were too fast for the interior fields to compensate. They felt like the buffeting of waves; and each time the noise that sang in the hull was more shrill and windy.

Four dozen bodies hurled together could have meant broken bones or worse. But two people, trained and alert, could keep their feet with the aid of a handrail. And it was needful that they do so. In this hour, folk must have before their sight a man and a woman who stood together unbowed.

Ingrid Lindgren completed her account. ' -- that is what is happening. We will not be able to stop before the death of the universe.'

The muteness into which she had spoken seemed to

deepen. A few women wept, a few men shaped oaths or prayers, but none was above a sough. In the front row, Captain Telander bent his head and covered his face. The ship lurched in another squall. Sound passed by, throbbing, groaning, whistling.

Lindgren's fingers momentarily clasped Reymont's. 'The constable has something to tell you,' she said.

He trod forward. Sunken and reddened, his eyes appeared to regard them in such ferocity that Chi-Yuen herself dared make no gesture. His tunic was wolf-gray, and besides his badge he wore his automatic pistol, the ultimate emblem. He said, quietly though with none of the first officer's compassion:

'I know you think this is the end. We've tried, and failed, and you should be left alone to make your peace with yourselves or your God. Well, I don't say you shouldn't do that. I have no firm idea what is going to become of us. I don't believe anyone can predict any more. Nature is turning too alien for that. In honesty, I agree that our chances look poor.

'But I don't think they are zero, either. And by this I don't mean that we can survive in a dead universe. That's the obvious thing to attempt. Slow down till our time rate isn't extremely different from outside, while continuing to move fast enough that we can collect hydrogen for fuel. Then spend what years remain in our bodies aboard this ship, never glancing out into the dark around us, never thinking about the fate of the child who'll soon be born.

'Maybe that's physically possible, if the thermodynamics of a collapsing space doesn't play tricks on us. I don't imagine that it's psychologically possible, however. Your expressions show you agree with me. Correct?

'What can we do?'

'I think we have a duty – to the race that begot us, to the children we might yet bring forth ourselves – a duty to keep trying, right to the finish.

'For most of you, that won't involve more than continuing to live, continuing to stay sane. I'm well aware that that could be as hard a task as human beings ever undertook.

The crew and the scientists who have relevant specialties will, in addition, have to carry on the work of the ship and of preparing for what's to come. It will be difficult.

'So make your peace. Interior peace. That's the only kind which ever existed anyway. The exterior fight goes on. I propose we wage it with no thought of surrender.'

Abruptly his words rang loud: 'I propose we go on to the next cycle of the cosmos.'

That snatched them to attention. Above a collective gasp and inarticulate cries, a few stridencies could be made out: ' – No! Lunacy!' – 'Great!' – 'Impossible!' – 'Blasphemy!' Reymont drew his gun and fired. The shot shocked them into quiet.

He grinned. 'Blank cartridge,' he said. 'Better than a gavel. Naturally, I discussed this beforehand with the officers and the astronomical experts. The officers, at least, agree the gamble is worth taking, if only because we haven't much to lose. But equally naturally, we want general accord. Let's discuss this in regular fashion. Captain Telander, will you preside?'

'No,' said the master faintly. 'You. Please.'

'Very well. Comments . . . ah, probably our senior physicist should begin.'

Ben-Zvi declared, in an almost indignant voice: 'The universe took between one and two hundred billion years to complete its expansion. It won't collapse in less time. Do you seriously believe we can acquire a tau that lets us outlive the cycle?'

'I seriously believe we should try,' Reymont answered. The ship trembled and belled. 'We gained a few per cent right there, in that galactic cluster. As matter gets more dense, we accelerate faster. Space itself is being pulled into a tighter and tighter curve. We couldn't circumnavigate the universe before, because it didn't last that long, in the form we knew it. But we should be able to circle the shrinking universe repeatedly. That's the opinion of Professor Chidambaran. Would you like to explain, Mohandas?'

'If you wish,' the cosmologist said. 'Time as well as space must be taken into reckoning. The characteristics of the whole continuum will change quite radically. Conservative assumptions lead me to the conclusion that, in effect, our present exponential decrease of the tau factor with respect to ship's time should itself increase to a higher order.' He paused. 'At a rough estimate, I would say that the time we experience under those circumstances, from now to the ultimate collapse, will be three months.'

Into the hush that followed another rustle of stupefaction, he added: 'Nevertheless, as I told the officers when they asked me to make this calculation, I do not see how we can survive. Our present observations vindicate the empirical proofs that Elof Nilsson found, these many eons ago in the Solar System, that the universe does indeed oscillate. It will be reborn. But first all matter and energy must be collected in a monobloc of the highest possible density and temperature. We might pass through a star at our current velocity and not be harmed. We can scarcely pass through the primordial nucleon. My personal suggestion is that we cultivate serenity.' He folded his hands in his lap.

'Not a bad idea,' Reymont said. 'But I don't think that's the sole thing we should do. We should keep flying also. Let me tell you what I told the original discussion group. Nobody disputed it.

'The fact is, nobody knows for sure what's going to happen. My guess is that everything will not get squeezed into a single zero-point Something. That's the kind of oversimplification which helps our math along but never does tell a whole story. I think the central core of mass is bound to have an enormous hydrogen envelope, even before the explosion. The outer parts of that envelope may not be too hot or radiant or dense for us. Space will be small enough, though, that we can circle around and around the monobloc as a kind of satellite. When it blows up and space starts to expand again, we'll spiral out ourselves. I know this is a sloppy way of phrasing, but it hints at what we can perhaps do. . . . Norbert?'

'I never thought of myself as a religious man,' Williams said. It was odd and disturbing to see him humbled. 'But this is too much. We're – well, what are we? Animals. My

God – very literally, my God – we can't go on . . . having regular bowel movements . . . while creation happens!'

Beside him, Emma Glassgold looked startled, then determined. Her hand shot aloft. Reymont recognized her.

'Speaking as a believer myself,' she announced, 'I must say that that is sheer nonsense. I'm sorry, Norbert, dear, but it is. God made us the way He wanted us to be. There's nothing shameful about any part of His handiwork. I would like to watch Him fashion new stars, and praise Him, as long as He sees fit that I should.'

'Good for you!' Ingrid Lindgren called.

'I might add,' Reymont said, 'I being a man with no poetry in his soul, and I suspect no soul to keep the poetry in . . . I might suggest you people look into yourselves and ask what psychological twists make you unwilling to live through the moment when time begins over. Isn't there, down inside, some identification with – your parents, maybe? You shouldn't see your parents in bed, therefore you shouldn't see a new cosmos begotten. Now that doesn't make sense.' He drew breath. 'We can't deny what's about to happen is awesome. But so is everything else. Always. I never thought stars were more mysterious, or had more magic, than flowers.'

Others wanted to talk. Eventually everyone did. Their sentences threshed wearily around and around the point. It was not to no purpose. They had to unburden themselves. But by the time they could finally adjourn the meeting, after a unanimous vote to proceed, Reymont and Lindgren were near a collapse of their own.

They did seize a moment's low-speaking privacy, as the people broke into groups and the ship roared with the hollow noise of her passage. She took both his hands and said: 'How I want to be your woman again.'

He stammered in gladness, 'Tomorrow? We, we'd have to move personal gear . . . and explain to our partners. . . . Tomorrow, my Ingrid?'

'No,' she answered. 'You didn't let me finish. All of me wants to, but I can't.'

Stricken, he asked, 'Why?'

'We mustn't risk it. The emotional balance is too fragile. Anything might let hell loose in any one of us. Elof and Ai-Ling would take it hard that we left – when death is this near.'

'She and he could – ' Reymont chopped off in mid-word. 'No. He could. She would. But no.'

'You wouldn't be the man I lie awake nights wishing for, if you could ask that of her. She never let you talk about those hours she gave us, did she?'

'No. How did you guess?'

'I didn't guess. I know her. And I won't have her do it again for us, Carl. Once was right. It won us back what we'd built together. Oftener, by stealth, is not any way to treat that thing.' Lindgren's speech stiffened into practicalities. 'Besides, Elof. He needs me. He blames himself, his advice, for letting us run the ship too long – as if any mortal man could have known! If he should learn that I – The desperation, maybe the suicide of a single individual could bring the whole crew down in hysteria.'

She straightened, faced him squarely, smiled, and said, her tone soft again: 'Afterward, yes. When we are safe. I'll never let you go then.'

'We may never be safe,' he protested. 'Chances are we won't. I want you back before I die.'

'And I you. But we can't. We mustn't. They depend on you. Absolutely. You're the only man who can lead us through what lies ahead. You've given me courage till I can help you a little. Nevertheless . . . Carl, it was never easy to be a king.'

She wheeled and walked from him.

He stood for a space, alone. Somebody approached the stage with a question. He waved the somebody aside. 'Tomorrow,' he said. Springing to the deck, he made his way to Chi-Yuen, who awaited him at the door.

She told him in an almost matter-of-fact voice: 'If we die with the last stars, Charles, I will still have had more from my life than I ever hoped, knowing you. What can I do for you?'

He regarded her. The ship's wild singing closed them off

from the rest of humanity. 'Come back to our cabin with me,' he said.

'Nothing else?'

'No, except to be what you are.' He ran fingers through his gray-shot hair. Awkward and puzzled, he said: 'I can't make fine phrases, Ai-Ling, and I'm not experienced in fine emotions. Tell me, is it possible to love two different people at once?'

She embraced him. 'Of course it is, silly.' Her answer was muffled by his flesh and less steady than before. But when she took his arm and they started for their quarters, she was smiling.

'Do you know,' she added at length, 'I wonder if the biggest surprise in these next months isn't how stubbornly ordinary life will keep on being.'

CHAPTER 21

Margarita's daughter was born in the night. No suns remained visible. The ship rolled through gales and thunder. While the birth took place, the father was bossing a work gang, and straining his own muscles, to further strengthen the hull. The baby's first cry responded to the noise of inward-falling worlds.

Things quieted down for a time afterward. The scientists had observed and computed until they understood something about those strange forces galloping through the light-years. Reprogrammed, the robots got the ship to sailing with the winds and vortices more often than across them.

Not everyone was in the mood to celebrate with a party, but those were whom Johann Freiwald and Jane Sadler invited. By dimming lights, she reduced the corner of the gym which they used to a room small and warm. This brought into vivid relief the Halloween ornaments she had hung up.

'Is that wise?' Reymont asked when he arrived with Chi-Yuen.

'We're not far off from the date by the calendar,' Sadler replied. 'Why not combine the occasions? Me, I think the jack o' lanterns add a touch of color we sure can use.'

'They might be too reminding. Not of Earth, maybe – I suppose we're getting over that – but, of, uh – '

'Yeh, it crossed my mind. A shipful of witches, devils, vampires, goblins, bogles, and spooks, screaming their way down the sky toward the Black Sabbath. Well, aren't we?' Sadler grinned and snuggled close to Freiwald. He laughed and hugged her. 'I feel exactly like doing that kind of nose thumbing.'

The rest agreed. They drank more than they were used to and got rowdy. At last they enthroned Boris Fedoroff on the stage, with a garland and a lei and two girls to wait on his every wish. Several other folk stood in a ring, arms linked, bawling out a song that had been ancient when the vessel left home.

> '*I makes no diff'rence where I end up when I die.*
> *It makes no diff'rence where I end up when I die.*
> > *Up to heaven or down to hell come,*
> > *I've got friends who'll make me welcome.*
> *It makes no diff'rence where I end up when I die.*'

Michael O'Donnell, entering late after his watch ended – there were live stand-bys at every stress point, these days – pushed through the crowd. 'Hey, Boris!' he called. The racket drowned him out.

> '*– Oh, you've got no use for money when you die.*
> > *For St Peter wants no ticket*
> > *When you stand at heaven's wicket.*
> *Oh, you've got no use for money when you die.*'

He reached the stage. 'Hey, Boris! Congratulations!'

> *'You shall have my old bicycle when I die.*
> *You shall have – '*

'Thank you,' Fedoroff boomed. 'Mainly Margarita's work. She runs quite a shipyard, no?'

> *'For the final kilometer*
> *Goes on tandem with St. Peter. – '*

'What will you name the kid?' O'Donnell asked.

> *'I'll shoot craps with old St. Peter when I die. – '*

'Haven't decided yet,' Fedoroff said. He waved a bottle. 'I can tell you, though, it won't be Eve.'

> *'If I shoot as I've shot here – '*

'Embla?' Ingrid Lindgren suggested. 'The first woman in the Eddic story.'

> *'I can take him for a beer.'*

'Not that either,' Fedoroff said.

> *'I'll shoot craps with old St. Peter when I die.'*

'Nor Leonora Christine,' the engineer went on. 'She's not going to be any damned symbol. She's going to be herself.' The singers began dancing in a circle.

> *'It's not certain we'll get liquor when we die.*
> *It's not certain we'll get liquor when we die.*
> *Let us then drink hell for leather*
> *Now tonight when we're together.*
> *It's not certain we'll get liquor when we die.'*

Chidambaran and Foxe-Jameson seemed dwarfed by the sprawling masses of the observatory apparatus, and artless amidst its meters and controls and flickering indicator lights, and loud and clumsy in the humming stillness that pervaded this deck. They rose when Captain Telander appeared.

'You asked me to come?' he said pointlessly. His wasted features set. 'What news? We've had calm this past month. . . .'

'That won't last.' Foxe-Jameson spoke half in exultation. 'Elof's gone in person to fetch Ingrid. We couldn't do that for you, sir. The image is still very faint, might get lost if we don't ride herd. You should be the first to know.' He returned to his chair before an electronic console. A screen above it showed darkness.

Telander shuffled close. 'What have you found?'

Chidambaran took him by the elbow and pointed at the screen. 'There. Do you see?'

On the edge of perception gleamed the dimmest and tiniest of sparks.

'A good ways off, naturally,' Foxe-Jameson said into the silence. 'We'll want to maintain a most respectful distance.'

'What is it?' Telander quavered.

'The germ of the monobloc,' Chidambaran answered. 'The new beginning.'

Telander stood long and long, staring, before he went to his knees. The tears ran quietly down his face. 'Father, I thank Thee,' he said.

Rising: 'And I thank you, gentlemen. Whatever happens next . . . we have come this far, we have done this much. I think I can carry on again . . . after what you have just shown me.'

When he finally left to return to the bridge, he walked with the stride of a commander.

Leonora Christine shouted, shuddered, and leaped.

Space flamed around her, a firestorm, hydrogen aglow from that supernal sun which was forming at the heart of existence, which burned brighter and brighter as the galaxies rained down into it. The gas hid the central travail behind sheets, banners, and spears of radiance, aurora, flame, lightning. Forces, unmeasurably vast, tore through and through the atmosphere: electric, magnetic, gravitational, nuclear fields; shock waves bursting across megaparsecs; tides and currents and cataracts. On the fringes of creation, through billion-year cycles which passed as moments, the ship of man flew.

Flew.

There was no other word. As far as humanity was concerned, or the most swiftly computing and reacting of machines, she fought a hurricane – but such a hurricane as had not been known since last the stars were melted together and hammered afresh.

'*Ya-a-ah-h-h!*' screamed Lenkei, and rode the ship down the trough of a wave whose crest shook loose a foam of supernovae. The haggard men on the steering bridge with him stared into the screen that had been built for this hour. What raged in it was not reality – present reality transcended any picturing or understanding – but a display of exterior force fields. It burned and roiled and spewed great sparks and globes. It believed in the metal of the ship, in flesh and skulls.

'Can't you stand any more?' Reymont shouted from his own seat. 'Barrios, relieve him.'

The other jet man shook his head. He was too stunned, too beaten from his previous watch.

'Okay.' Reymont unharnessed himself. 'I'll try. I've handled a lot of different types of craft.' No one heard him through the fury around, but all saw him fight across the pitching, whirling deck. He took the auxiliary control chair, on the opposite side of Lenkei from Barrios, and laid his mouth close to the pilot's ear. 'Phase me in.'

Lenkei nodded. Together their hands moved across the board.

They must hold *Leonora Christine* well away from the growing monobloc, whose radiation would otherwise surely kill them; at the same time, they must stay where the gas was so dense that tau could continue to decrease for them, turning these final phoenix gigayears into hours; and they must keep the ship riding safely through a chaos that, did it ever strike her full on, would rip her into nuclear particles. No computers, no instruments, no precedents might guide them. It must be done on instinct and trained reflex.

Gradually Reymont entered the pattern, until he could steer alone. The rhythms of rebirth were wild, but they were there. Ease on starboard . . . vector at nine o'clock low . . . now *push* that thrust! . . . brake a little here . . .

don't let her broach . . . swing wide of that flame cloud if you can. . . . Thunder brawled. The air was sharp with ozone, and cold.

The screen blanked. An instant later, every fluoropanel in the ship turned simultaneously ultraviolet and infrared, and blackness plunged down. Those who lay harnessed alone, throughout the hull, heard invisible lightnings walk the corridors. Those in command bridge, pilot bridge, engine room, who manned the ship, felt a heaviness greater than planets – they could not move, nor stop a movement once begun – and then felt a lightness such that their bodies began to shake asunder – and this was a change in inertia itself, in every constant of nature as space-time-matter-energy underwent its ultimate convulsion – for a moment infinitesimal and infinite, men, women, child, ship, and death were one.

It passed, so swiftly that they could not tell if it had been. Light came back, and outside vision. The storm grew fiercer. But now through it, seen distorted so that they appeared to be blue-white firedrops that broke into sparks as they flew, fountaining off in two huge curving sheets, now came the nascent galaxies.

The monobloc had exploded. Creation had begun.

Reymont went over to full deceleration. *Leonora Christine* started slowly to slow; and she flew out into a reborn light.

CHAPTER 22

Boudreau and Nilsson nodded at each other. They grinned. 'Yes, indeed,' the astronomer said.

Reymont looked restlessly around the observatory. 'Yes, what?' he demanded. He jerked one thumb at a visual screen. Space swarmed with little dancing incandescences. 'I can see for myself. The galactic groups are still close together. Most of them are still nothing but hydrogen nebulae. And hydrogen atoms are still thick between them, comparatively speaking. What of it?'

'Computation on the basis of data,' Boudreau said. 'I have been consulting with the team leaders here. We felt you deserved as well as needed to hear in confidence what we have learned, so that you might make the decision.'

Reymont stiffened. 'Lars Telander is the captain.'

'Yes, yes. Nobody wants to go behind his back, especially when he is once more doing a superb job with the ship. The folk within the ship, though, they are another matter. Be realistic, Charles. You know what you are to them.'

Reymont folded his arms. 'Well, proceed, then.'

Nilsson went into lecture gear. 'Never mind details,' he said. 'This result came out of the problem you set us, to find in which directions the matter was headed, and which the antimatter. You recall, we were able to do this by tracing the paths of plasma masses through the magnetic fields of the universe as a whole while its radius was small. And thereby the officers were enabled to bring this vessel safely into the matter half of the plenum.

'Now in the course of making those studies, we collected and processed an astonishing amount of data. And here is what else we have come up with. The cosmos is new and in some respects disordered. Things have not yet sorted themselves out. Within a short range of us, compared to distances we have already traversed, are material complexes – galaxies and protogalaxies -- with every possible velocity.

'We can use that fact to our advantage. That is, we can pick the clan, family, cluster, and individual galaxy we want to make our destination – pick one at which we can arrive with zero relative speed at any point of its evolution that we choose. Within fairly wide limits, anyhow. We couldn't get to a galaxy which is more than about fifteen billion years old by the time we reach it: not unless we wanted to approach it circuitously. Nor can we overtake any before it is about one billion years old. But otherwise we can choose what we like.

'And . . . whatever we elect, the maximum shipboard time required to come there, braked, will be no longer than weeks!'

Reymont said an amazed obscenity.

'You see,' Nilsson explained, 'we can select a target whose velocity will be almost identical with ours when we fetch it.'

'Oh yes,' Reymont mumbled. 'I can see that. I'm just not used to having luck in our favor.'

'Not luck,' Nilsson said. 'Given an oscillating universe, this development was inevitable. Or so we perceive by hindsight. We need merely use the fact.'

'Best you decide on our goal,' Boudreau urged. 'Now. Those other idiots, they would wrangle for hours, if you put it to a vote. And every hour means untold cosmic time lost, which reduces our options. If you will tell us what you want, I'll plot an appropriate course and the ship can start off on it very shortly. The captain will take your recommendation. The rest of our people will accept any *fait accompli* you hand them, and thank you for it. You know that.'

Reymont paced for some turns. His boots clacked on the deck. He rubbed his brow, where the wrinkles lay deep. Finally he confronted his interlocutors. 'We want more than a galaxy,' he said. 'We want a planet to live on.'

'Understood,' Nilsson agreed. 'May I speak for a planet – a system – of the same approximate age as Earth had? Say, five billion years? It seems to take about that long for a fair probability of the kind of biosphere we like having evolved. We could live in a Mesozoic type of environment, I imagine, but we would rather not.'

'Seems reasonable,' Reymont nodded. 'How about metals, though?'

'Ah, yes. We want a planet as rich in heavy elements as Earth was. Not too much less, or an industrial civilization will be hard to establish. Not too much more, or we could find numerous areas where the soil is poisonous. Since higher elements are formed in the earlier generations of stars, we should look for a galaxy that will be as old, at rendezvous, as ours was.'

185

'No,' Reymont said. 'Younger.'

'*Hein?*' Boudreau blinked.

'We can probably find a planet like Earth, also with respect to metals, in a young galaxy,' Reymont said. 'A globular cluster ought to have plenty of supernovae in its early stages, which ought to enrich the interstellar medium locally, giving second-generation G-type suns about the same composition as Sol. As we enter our target galaxy, let's scout for that kind.'

'We may not detect any that we can reach in less than years,' Nilsson warned.

'Well, then we don't,' Reymont answered. 'We can settle for a planet less well-endowed with iron and uranium than Earth was. That's not crucial. We have the technology to make do with light alloys and organics. We have hydrogen fusion for power.

'The important thing is that we be about the first intelligent race alive in those parts.'

They stared at him.

He smiled in a way they had not seen before. 'I'd like us to have our pick of worlds, when our descendants get around to interstellar colonization,' he said. 'And I'd like us to become – oh, the elders. Not imperialists; that's ridiculous; but the people who were there from the beginning and know their way around, and are worth learning from. Never mind what physical shape the younger races have. Who cares? But let's make this, as nearly as possible, a human galaxy, in the widest sense of the word "human." Maybe even a human universe.

'I think we've earned that right.'

Leonora Christine took only three months of her people's lives from the moment of creation to the moment when she found her home.

That was partly good fortune but also due to forethought. The newborn atoms had burst outward with a random distribution of velocities. Thus, in the course of ages, they formed hydrogen clouds which attained distinct individualities. While they drifted apart, these clouds condensed into

186

sub-clouds – which, under the slow action of many forces, differentiated themselves into separate families, then single galaxies, then individual suns.

But inevitably, in the early stages, exceptional situations occurred. Galaxies were as yet near to each other. They still contained anomalous groups. Thus they exchanged matter. A large star cluster might form within one galaxy, but having more than escape velocity, might cross to another (with stars coalescing in it meanwhile) that could capture it. In this way, the variety of stellar types belonging to a particular galaxy was not limited to those that it could have evolved at its own age.

Zeroing in on her destination, *Leonora Christine* kept watch for a well-developed cluster whose speed she could easily match. And as she entered its domain, she looked for a star of the right characteristics, spectral and velocital. To nobody's surprise, the nearest of that sort had planets. She decelerated toward it.

The procedure differed from the original scheme, which had been to go by at high speed, making observations while she passed through the system. Reymont was responsible for it. This once, he said, let a chance be taken. The odds weren't too bad. Measurements made across light-years with the instruments and techniques developed aboard ship gave reason to expect that a certain attendant of that yellow sun might offer a haven to man.

If not – a year would have been lost, the year required to reapproach *c* with respect to the entire galaxy. But if there actually was a planet such as lived in memory, no further deceleration would be called for. Two years would have been gained.

The gamble seemed worthwhile. Given twenty-five fertile couples, an extra two years meant an extra half hundred ancestors for the future race.

Leonora Christine found her world, the very first time.

CHAPTER 23

On a hill that viewed wide across a beautiful valley, a man stood with his woman.

Here was not New Earth. That would have been too much to expect. The river far below them was tinted gold with tiny life, and ran through meadows whose many-fronded growth was blue. Trees looked as if they were feathered, in shades of the same color, and the wind set some kinds of blossoms in them to chiming. It bore scents which were like cinnamon, and iodine, and horses, and nothing for which men had a name. On the opposite side lifted stark palisades, black and red, fanged with crags, where flashed the horns of a glacier.

Yet the air was warm; and humankind could thrive here. Enormous above river and ridges towered clouds which shone silver in the sun.

Ingrid Lindgren said, 'You mustn't leave her, Carl. She deserves too well of us.'

'What are you talking about?' Reymont retorted. 'We can't leave each other. None of us can. Ai-Ling understands you're something unique to me. But so is she, in her own way. So are we all, everyone to everyone else. Aren't we? After what we've been through together?'

'Yes. It's only – I never thought to hear those words from you, Carl, darling.'

He laughed. 'What did you expect?'

'Oh, I don't know. Something harsh and unyielding.'

'The time for that is over,' he said. 'We've got where we were going. Now we have to start afresh.'

'Also with each other?' she asked, a little teasingly.

'Yes. Of course. Good Lord, hasn't this been discussed enough among the bunch of us? We'll need to take from the past what's good and forget what was bad. Like .. well, the whole question of jealously simply isn't relevant. There'll be no later immigrants. We have to share our genes around as much as we can. Fifty of us to start a whole intelligent species over again! So your worry about someone being hurt, or left out, or anything – it doesn't arise. With all the work ahead of us, personalities have no importance whatsoever.'

He pulled her to him and chuckled down at her. 'Not that we can't tell the universe Ingrid Lindgren is the loveliest object in it,' he said, threw himself down under a tall old tree, and tugged her hand. 'Come here. I told you we were going to take a holiday.'

Steely-scaled, with a skirling along its wings, passed overhead one of those creatures called dragons.

Lindgren joined Reymont, but hesitantly. 'I don't know if we should, Carl,' she said.

'Why not?'

'Too much to do.'

'Construction, planting, everything's coming along fine. The scientists haven't reported any menace, actual or potential, that we can't deal with. We can well afford to loaf a bit.'

'All right, let's face the fact.' She brought the words unwillingly forth. 'Kings get no holidays.'

'What *are* you babbling about?' Reymont lounged back against the rough, sweet-scented bole and rumpled her hair, which was bright beneath the young sun. After dark there would be three moons to shine upon her, and more stars in the sky than men had known before.

'You,' she said. 'They look to you, the man who saved them, the man who dared survive, they look to you for – '

He interrupted her in the most enjoyable way.

'Carl!' she protested.

'Do you mind?'

'No. Certainly not. On the contrary. But – I mean, your work – '

'My work,' he said, 'is my share of the community's job. No more and no less. As for any other position: They had a proverb in America which went, "If nominated, I will not run; if elected, I will not serve." '

She looked at him with a kind of terror. 'Carl! You can't mean that!'

'I sure as hell can,' he answered. For a moment he turned serious again. 'Once a crisis is past, once people can manage for themselves . . . what better can a king do for them than take off his crown?'

Then he laughed, and made her laugh with him, and they were merely human.